D1367511

I WAS LUCKY ENOUGH TO BE GIVEN
TWO MOMS. THIS BOOK IS FOR BOTH
OF THEM. FOR MY MOM KAY AND MY
MOTHER-IN-LAW CYNTHIA.

SOMETIMES IT'S THE SMALLEST
DECISIONS THAT CAN CHANGE YOUR
LIFE FOREVER.
-KERI RUSSELL

One

7 YEARS EARLIER

H OW THE FLYING HELL DID I GET HERE? *No, I don't mean physically; I mean in the metaphorical sense. Hell, for all I know all of this could be in my head.*

It'd been I don't know how many hours since I've had my last fix. My body was aching horrendously and the high was completely gone at this point. I was itching. The only thing that would help was the one thing that I knew was slowly killing me. But that didn't really matter. Even if I had a needle full of my demise, I would still be tied up sitting on this stained and filthy mattress.

Heroin had been my drug of choice since I was about sixteen years old. Now, I'm eighteen and I have no illusions that I will make it to see my nineteenth birthday. My stupid-ass addiction got me in this situation and now I had to figure out a way out of it. *Even if I can somehow get out of this, where would I go?* I

1

had no family; they abandoned me years ago. Well, the ones who didn't abuse me, anyway. I had to figure out how to get away from all of this.

I made a huge tactical error. I tried to outsmart a drug dealer and failed so miserably it was nearing comical — to someone, not me though. *What the fuck was I thinking?* I took loan after loan from Reggie and then, when my time to pay up came, I ran. I didn't have the money to pay him. I lied and told him I was getting his money, but, yeah, it didn't work. So there I sat, tied up praying he kills me or shows mercy and gives me another fix. *Yeah, mercy, what an epic joke.* Reggie wouldn't know the meaning of the word if it walked up to him and took a shit on his face.

Reggie was a fifty-something dirt bag drug dealer. Unlike me, he was always tidy and clean. His black hair was always tightly slicked to his grease ball skull. He was about six foot tall with a fairly slim build. His face was craggy and covered with wrinkles and old acne scars. In short, he was a total sleaze-ball who thought himself a businessman.

I flopped over on the dirty mattress. My hands were bound behind my back and my feet were tied at the ankles. I looked like a calf tied up at a rodeo. Even my abilities wouldn't help me now. *I am a pusher, or I was anyway.* A human who has genetic anomalies that pushed the human race forward. I was crazy fast and had some telekinetic abilities. After years of martial arts, I should have had better control over my abilities. But with years of drug use, I might as well have had no abilities other than finding a vein. Another wave of pain hit me and I curled into a tight ball. *I will not throw up, I won't. I just won't.*

I heard footsteps outside the room I was kept in. And I use the term *room* loosely, as it was more like a closet. The steps were distant and seemed to echo off the sides of my skull. With just the sound of them I thought my ears were bleeding. Drugs. The steps had to lead to my sweet release. Maybe I'd OD and die. I was too much of a coward to do the job myself.

The door creaked open. The sound was pure agony. God, it was like an ice pick was being jabbed into my brain. *Why is that door so damned loud? Don't they have some WD-40? Oh shit.* The walls started spinning. I was going to lose it. I clenched my teeth and swallowed the bile back. When I thought I could see the world again without tossing my cookies, I cracked my eyes open to see I was face down on the mattress. I turned my head to breathe in cool air, trying to clear the cotton that seemed to have taken up residence in my head. Just as I did, I felt a strong hand grasp the rat's nest I call hair and pull up, dragging me to my feet. Pain exploded in my head and behind my eyes. I went blind for a few heartbeats. *Crap, that fucking hurts.*

"Addison, oh little Addy." Reggie's voice seemed to ooze around me and coil around my stomach.

"Reggie, don't call me that," I intoned in my sweetest southern drawl. There was only one person in my life who cared about me enough to call me Addy, and that sure as shit wasn't Reggie. He probably charged his own mother rent.

His grip tightened on my hair as he yanked me to look at him. My feet were barely touching the floor.

"Little Addison, you're hardly in any position to be arguing with me." He licked his lips. The gesture made my stomach turn. His mouth was so close to mine when he spoke I could smell the stale garlic on his breath. "Now, what am I going to do with you, my little junkie? I gave you so many chances because you're just so pretty. But, then you run when payment is due? Tisk, tisk, my little pusher."

His tongue flicked out of his mouth and traced my bottom lip in a painfully slow motion. *If I am going to hurl, now would be a great time.* I knew if I bit him or spit on him he would do far worse things to me. Had I not been on so many drugs, I could use my abilities to get me out of this. But, no, he was right; I was a junkie. "Addison, you are so beautiful. I know how I want my money back. I want to take it out of your body."

Oh God. The thought of his body anywhere near mine made the bile rise in my throat and splash the back of my mouth. *If I am going to die, let it be before his nasty hands touch me.*

"Such a shame my boss wants to meet my little pusher," he said, stroking a finger along my jaw.

Finally, blessedly, he let my hair go. I crumpled to the floor in a shaking heap. *Who the hell is his boss and why would he care about me?* My head was throbbing; oh wait, belay that, the whole world was throbbing. Pain exploded on the right side of my ribcage. My breath went out in a whoosh and I knew ribs had to have been cracked, if not broken. I curled in on myself, trying to make myself a smaller target.

"Get up, you worthless piece of shit. Or I will take some pleasure from your body. And baby, trust me, it will be all pain for you." He kicked me; Christ, the asshole had kicked me. Didn't he know I was going through withdrawal and I didn't need any more of his bullshit? I tried to take in as much air as I could but it wasn't nearly as much as I would have liked. My ribs prevented me from breathing in more. I shifted my weight to my shins and lifted my body up into a kneeling position, looking up to find the dirt bag watching me. *Asshole.*

My blue gaze met his shit-brown eyes and I gave him a sweet smile and questioned, "If it pleases his majesty, would you help me out here?"

His smile was all teeth and predator, "Not unless it's my cock in your face." *Um ew!* Who talked to people like that?

I looked around and finally spotted the bed next to me. I placed my face and upper body on the bed and pushed down, lifting my ass in the air. Not my best look but hey, I did have a nice ass. Clearly, I wasn't the only one who thought so because I felt Reggie's hand slide down the right cheek and toward my ...

I stood up abruptly and far too fast for my addled head. But, there was no way in hell I was letting this ass munch touch me anywhere, much less there. I swayed a bit, but after a moment I was as steady as I could expect. He bent down and cut the zip ties that bound my ankles. Even that small freedom felt like a victory.

I felt Reggie's hand on the center of my back and then I was pushed so far forward I almost fell again. "Walk."

"Okay, but I don't know where I'm going. Christ, Reggie, I'm withdrawing so either deal with me being sluggish and feeling like shit or let me shoot up." I was hoping, begging. Fuck, I was praying for the latter. *Praying to God to shoot up; shit, Addison, that's messed up even from you.*

"Oh no, my pretty pusher, no more freebies. Time to pay up." His tone said he had an idea of the type of payment his boss had in mind. *Please, please don't vomit.* But, if I did, I was aiming for Reggie's shoes.

We walked, and by walk I mean I shuffled at a snail's pace, for what seemed like three miles. But, things like time and distance were so muddled. We were in a building of some kind. There were offices behind closed oak doors. There was crown molding on the ceiling and rich blue carpet. I must have been in the basement of this place because the scent of mold that had been so prominent in my little cell was somewhat muted here. We arrived at an elevator and Reggie pushed the up button. Immediately the door popped open with a ding. *I never have that kind of luck.* If I had pushed the button we would have to wait for twenty freaking minutes.

The elevator was tiled in white marble and gold. *Shit, where are we?* Reggie hit the top button that read twenty-six. Right on time began the music. I knew the song but there was no way with my fried brain I could have said what it was.

The whole ride only took a minute or so, but with every passing floor my heartbeat picked up the pace. By the twenty-sixth floor my heart was a fraction of a degree from exploding. When the doors slid open we got out to see nothing but white marble floors and glass walls. Reggie took my arm and led me only a few steps to another elevator. He again pushed the up button and, like magic, the door opened. I couldn't help but scowl at him. *Rat bastard.* We stepped in and there were no buttons to push, only a key hole. *Weird.* Reggie pulled a small gold key out of his pocket and slipped it into the panel. Just above the keyhole there were two ornate letters etched on to the surface: CB. Fear like none I have ever felt licked its cold slimy tongue along my spine. I had a bad feeling I knew who CB was. If it was who I thought, I would be so screwed and would have to pray for an easy death.

We stood in front of a frosted glass door with two huge, ornate handles. On the door there were the same CB initials etched into the frosted glass as in the elevator. I felt Reggie's breath next to my ear as he whispered, "Afraid yet? You should be." Hell yes I was afraid. I may have wet my panties I was so damned afraid. But, I wasn't going to tell him that.

No one knocked; we just stood there waiting. Finally, after a small eternity, a short portly man in a too-tight suit pulled the door open. He reminded me of Santa without the beard. Santa looked at me and found me really lacking. *Yeah well, me too, buddy.* He motioned for us to walk into the huge open room off to the left of the door. The room was all white, from the lush carpet to the walls to the furniture. And the size of the room, Jesus, it had to be bigger than any apartment I had ever lived in.

"You may sit. The Master will be with you soon." Santa did not sound like any Santa I recalled hearing. His voice was flat and without any type of inflection. *Creepy.*

I looked around at the white room and then glanced down at myself. I had on baggy ripped jeans and who knew the last time they were washed, a used-to-be-white tank top that had holes and mystery stains on it. *Is one of the straps of my shirt ripped? Shit.* I was a mess. My once blonde, now pink hair lay in a nest atop, wait no, on the side of my head. I only stood at five-foot-three and I couldn't weigh more than 105 pounds. That's what a diet of Cheetos and drugs will do for you. I glanced back at the white room. *Yeah, I'll stand.*

There were ornate paintings on the walls and gold busts everywhere. There was so much money in this room alone it could pay my back rent and rent for ten years. I was staring at what had to be a reproduction Picasso when an involuntary shiver ran up my spine, but I refused to turn around. I felt a cold finger trace a line on the back of my neck and could not stop myself from shivering again. I turned around to come face to face with Cannon Blackwood, the master of all

Vampires. *Oh shit.*

Holy crap buckets, but he was handsome. He was no shorter than six foot six. His long, black hair was slicked back in a ponytail at the base of his neck. He had a long face and a large nose. On someone else it would look weird or too big, but on him it was perfect. He had a full mouth and a square chin, with a black beard that was kept very close and well maintained. But, under those lips I knew hid two very sharp teeth. Then there were his beautiful, dark, nearly black eyes. His body was lean, but I was willing to bet that if we took off that designer suit he had on, we would find a sculpted body colored like pale silk.

"Hello, little one." His accent was slightly eastern European and iced my blood to a standstill. He too sent an appraising glance over me, although I couldn't decipher his reaction. "Reginald, you did not tell me your pusher was such a small, pretty thing."

Was that a glint of fang I saw peeking through? This was the first Vampire I had seen in person. I wished I had enough brain power left to not gawk at him, but, alas, there was nothing there.

"Reginald, you may go," he spoke, never taking his eyes off of me.

"Sir, I would like to stay to see …" For once, Reggie's voice wavered. That SOB was scared. *Well, he should be.*

"I don't care in the least bit what you think, much less what you would like. Whatever debt she owes you will be paid. You will not come within one-hundred feet of her. Do I make myself clear?" Again, Cannon

9

said all of this without ever breaking eye contact with me. It was unnerving. It was like I was a puzzle and he was trying to figure me out.

"Yes, sir," Reggie stated in a tight tone. He swiftly exited. I didn't see him leave, only heard, as I could not take my eyes off the Vampire in front of me.

"You are too small. You need to eat," Cannon remarked finally, blessedly breaking eye contact. He began to walk in a tight circle around me.

"I can't eat when I can't pay for food." My voice was raspy, but it still had that southern twang it always held.

"Yet, you can afford to buy drugs from Reggie? You would rather destroy this beautiful body?" I heard a snick of a knife and flinched. *Oh, goodness, here I go.* He went behind me and cut the bonds on my wrists. *Yeah, a Vampire who killed with a knife, real smart, Addison.* He then moved around me and picked up my right arm and inspected it thoroughly. Then, when he was done, he did the same to my left. I knew what he was looking at. The track marks. I felt so exposed with this man near me. He moved his hand up my arm to my shoulder, then slipped a finger under my exposed bra strap and snapped it. I flinched, not from the pain, but from the ice his touch left behind.

"I never paid Reggie. Why do you think I'm in so much shit with him?" I didn't just say that, did I? Cannon's eyebrows shot up and a full-on smile splayed across his face. I glanced from his black eyes to his teeth and almost gasped in shock. There were no fangs. *What the hell?*

He leaned in next to my ear and whispered, "My fangs are only visible when I am hungry or express any other strong emotion." The mere closeness of him sent my knees a-knocking.

"Oh," was all I could manage. Cannon moved back and continued his tight circle path around me.

"Tell me, Addison Fitzpatrick, what push abilities do you possess?"

I didn't dare lie to this man. Hell, he had my full name, who knew what else he knew? "I am really fast. Not just running. I-I have quick reflexes, normally. I also have some telekinetic abilities. Though ..." I trailed off, not remembering what I was going to say. I began to sweat. *Fucking withdrawal.* I was going to need a major fix when this was over. If I lived.

"Though?" he reminded me gently.

I blinked my eyes rapidly to try to clear the fuzzy haze that was moving in. It was becoming harder for me to concentrate, especially with a shark circling me.

"Oh ... though I don't have much control over that ability."

"Interesting." He paused at my back. I felt a bead of sweat roll down my spine and pool there. Soon the shakes would come. "Do you know what Reggie would have done to you had I not said your debt would be paid?" He stayed at my back.

"I have an idea. He said he would have taken it out of my body." Ugh, just the thought repulsed me.

"Yes, I believe that would have happened." He moved closer to me, as I could feel the coolness radiating from his body. "If he would have offered you one more fix for you to get in bed with him, what would you have said?"

Now that pissed me off. I was fucking dirty, I had two broken ribs at least, and I wasn't even allowed to go to the bathroom. I turned around to face him and pointed a finger in his chest. I'd had it up to here with these assholes. "Look, buddy, I may be a lot of things. I know I'm a junkie, you don't need to remind me of that. And I have done some less-than-stellar things to get here. But, I would never and have never given my body freely to someone I haven't loved. I am not a whore." I was on drugs, I mean that would really be the only excuse I would have for doing and saying what I had to this man.

He stepped forward, closing the small distance between us, and asked, "What if I offered the same thing? You know what is at stake here, pusher."

I met his black eyes with my cool blue ones. "Not even for you."

Abruptly, he stepped away. "Good. I wouldn't want that awkwardness in the middle of our arrangement."

"A-a-arrangement?" I asked stupidly. Gosh, this guy was intense. And the most intense thing I could really handle right now was a bag of gummi bears.

"Yes, I did you a favor and now I want three in return," he asserted briskly. I bet he used the same tone when ordering bagels. *Does he eat bagels?*

"I'm sorry, I am going through some major withdrawal, but did you say I owe you three favors?"

12

What kind of game was he playing? Whatever it was, it wasn't funny.

"Yes, I believe I was quite clear. I did something for you with Reggie back there and now I want something from you."

"What could you want from me? I'm just a junkie pusher." I was honestly mystified as to what he could want. Last time I checked I wasn't a fucking genie.

"Oh, my little one, I want nothing from you now other than a yes. But there will come a time when I will collect on what you owe me. Also, clean yourself up. You're too pretty to be such a mess."

"So, let me get this straight. I will owe you three favors. And you will pick a time to collect but that won't be now because I am of no use to you now? Why am I of no use to you now?" I genuinely wanted to know. I tried desperately not to be offended but damn it, I was.

"My little pusher is feisty. You, dear, are of no use to yourself much less anyone else. Clean your life up. I will not have one of my tools so dirty." Again he spoke with a completely detached tone.

"I am not your tool." I was insulted. I mean, what did he think me as, a garden hoe?

"Once you say yes to this deal, you are mine. I will leave you on our own, but when I need you, you will have to come. You will be bound to me." His eyes flicked to my exposed neck then back to my eyes. I had no idea what being bound entitled, but it couldn't be roses and chocolate. *Shit.*

"What if I say no? If I say yes and I grant your three

wishes, am I free to go?"

He smiled at the mention of three wishes. "Yes, once you grant my three wishes you may go. And say no and I will give you back to Reggie so he may take his payment from you."

I thought about all of this, quickly realized there were no choices. I had gotten myself into this situation by being so damn messed up. I had a shitty childhood and let that turn my teen years into crap. I did not want to be a messed-up adult. I wanted to get back into martial arts and wanted to be able to pay my rent on time. But, most of all, I wanted to erase the track marks and the first eighteen years of my life. This insanely scary man was offering me a do over. *A mulligan.*

I looked up at his stone-filled gaze and uttered one word, the only word I could say, "Yes."

Two
PRESENT DAY

"So, ADDISON, I KNOW YOU ARE A MARTIAL ARTS badass and incredibly beautiful, but I would love to know more about you. What was your childhood like?" Kyle asked, just before he stuffed a slice of pizza in his mouth.

I did my best not to gag; watching people eat sometimes had this effect on me. Then his question hit me like a spinning hook kick to the face. *What a fucking joke of a question.* I honestly almost laughed at the damn guy. *Okay, Addison, what should we say?* Oh how about, *"Well, Kyle, funny you should ask, I bounced around from home to home because no one wanted me. My mother was an alcoholic who drank herself to death when I was three. The only person who did care, a brother, went missing when I was three. Finally, when I found a home for more than six months, horrible things happened and when I told my aunt, she kicked me out. Then, I was addicted to heroin for*

15

the majority of my teenage years. Oh and a Vampire owns me for the most part. Yeah, I didn't say any of that.

"Oh, you know, fairly normal. How about you?" And that, ladies and gentlemen, was why I didn't date. I didn't even know why I agreed to this stupid farce as it was. Peer pressure? Guilt? The fact I hadn't been on a date in four hundred years? Ugh!

Kyle was the father of a little girl in my class at the dojo. He was attractive, a good father, had a great job, and his little girl, Erica, was too cute for words. When I looked at him, I felt nothing. I mean, I wanted to feel something, but, alas, I felt like I was on a date with my cousin. Ew. The thought of that made me feel a little ill. I was twenty-five and I finally had my life together. I was teaching some classes in Tang Soo Do at the dojo and was able to pay my bills on time. Life had really never been better. Then some creature possessed me to say yes when Kyle asked me out on this date. *Oh shit, is he talking?*

"My parents divorced when I was ten. It wasn't all bad, you know. Double holidays and such," he said, grabbing another slice of pizza. "Do you not like the pizza? You haven't touched yours."

I looked down at the slice of untouched pizza. *What is wrong with me?* I should be fawning all over this guy. He was fairly handsome with his reddish-blond hair and dark-blue eyes. He was taller than me, not that that took much, about five foot eleven. He didn't seem to be ripped, but he was in shape. He had an adorable dimple on his left cheek. And there I sat, feeling nothing.

16

I mean, I really tried. I even got all dolled up. My long, blonde hair cascaded in waves past my shoulders. I had smoky makeup on. Hell, I had lipstick on. I never wear lipstick. I had a fairly muscular build, so I loved to show off my legs, but my arms I did my best to hide with makeup or a shawl. It was the middle of summer and in Atlanta that meant hot. I wore a blue baby doll cami with white short shorts. I was able to go without a bra, as my cup size was a B on a good day. I was short, but I had gained some much-needed weight over the last seven years and was pretty happy with my body. Especially my ass, and it looked pretty good in these shorts.

"Sorry, I got wrapped up in listening and forgot." I picked up the slice covered in jalapenos and took a bite. It was good but, much like this date, bland. Maybe there was something wrong with me? That had to be it. I was broken.

Kyle spent the rest of dinner talking. Who had that much to talk about? I swear to God I knew how the man took his coffee and his underwear size. Okay, maybe not, but shit he talked a lot. The only part where I didn't tune him out was when he was talking about Erica. I loved kids. I loved teaching them how to defend themselves and Erica was especially bright and talented when it came to Tang Soo Do.

Two painful hours later, we stood outside the building I called home. Would he try to kiss me? He seemed to be enjoying the date. I guess I was a talented actress. Possible new career option?

That's about when it happened. Kyle was saying he wanted to see me again when I felt like my stomach was being pulled from my body. I bent over in pain. My vision went white, then red, and then returned to normal. *Shit.* I was being pulled. It felt like I was shot with a harpoon and being yanked toward something. I had this happen one other time, about six years ago. When one was bound to a Vampire, that Vampire could pull you when you were needed.

"Addison, are you okay?" Kyle asked in a clearly concerned tone.

Last time this happened, I threw up. While I had no interest in Kyle, I also had no interest in losing my dinner on his loafers. *Loafers? Who wears loafers?* I groaned and stood up to meet his concerned gaze.

"Uh, yeah, I'm good. Stomach cramp. I-I need to go." Shit, the pulling sensation was getting stronger. *Fuck me. Why can't he use a cell phone like everyone else?* I turned, put my key in the door, and ran up the stairs. He was calling after me, but I couldn't make out what he uttered.

I fumbled with my keys at my door. After a small eternity, I busted through the door and scrambled over my couch to get to the kitchen. I tore open my junk drawer and turned it over on the counter. *Where the hell is it? Ah!* I grabbed my ID card and ran back out the door, almost forgetting to lock it behind me. I was going to be ripped apart if the pulling got any more intense. I flew down the stairs and about barged through Kyle.

"Shit, Kyle, what are you doing here?"

"I, uh, wanted to make sure you were okay. You just disappeared." His expression showed just how surprised he was by my speed. I really didn't have time for this.

"Kyle, I don't have time to explain, but I need to go." I tried to move past him, but he stepped in front of me. I really did not want to out myself as a pusher, but if this pulling got much worse, I wouldn't be given much choice. "Kyle, thank you for the great date. Please call me again. I would love to do this again, but I have to go. Someone needs me." It wasn't all a lie. This guy just wasn't getting the hint.

"Okay. I know you can protect yourself. Just be careful." I turned to jog down the sidewalk when he grabbed my hand and pulled it to his lips and kissed it. "I'll call you soon for another date."

I gently removed my hand from his and jogged away. *Yeah, you wish, buddy,* was what I wanted to say, but instead remarked, "Sure." As much as I wanted to turn him down for another date, I really didn't have time for all that. Once I rounded the corner, I kicked my pace up to high gear.

What looked like sprinting to most people was just a walk in the park to me. At my fastest, I am just a breeze to the people around me. I only needed to go about ten miles. As long as there weren't too many obstacles in my way, like people or mailboxes, I would be there in a few minutes. If it were a straight line, I'd be there in less than a minute.

It was about 9 p.m. and there weren't too many

people around with it being a school night. The middle of the city stayed pretty busy, but not with people on the sidewalks. Cars littered the streets, but that kept the people out of my way.

A few minutes later, I stood in front of Blackwood Tower. It was the largest building in downtown Atlanta. It was honestly a gaudy monstrosity that stuck out like a sore thumb in the Atlanta skyline. It made me wonder if Cannon Blackwood had some inadequacies he was making up for. Like his dick wasn't the biggest and most talented in Atlanta. And, of course, here I stood, his little bitch on an invisible leash. Another sharp pull on our connection left me bent over gasping for air. *What the hell is wrong with him? I know he knows I am here. Asshole.* I staggered to the doorman.

"Ma'am, are you okay?" the elderly man asked, as I used him to right myself. After a few moments, the pain turned into a dull throb. I pulled out my ID card and held it to the man.

"I will be when your fucking boss stops pulling me!" I was beyond snippy due to the fact that a crazy person was ripping me apart from the inside out. I mean, it was just rude at this point.

The man looked at my ID and stepped aside. I didn't even wait for him to open the door, I just ran through the doorway and straight to the elevator. I was so over being nice. The lobby, I assumed, was just as elaborate as the rest of the building, but, honestly, I was in a hurry to get this asshole to stop rubbing my lamp. I pressed the up button and waited. And, of course, I had to wait no less than five minutes for the damn thing to get down to the lobby floor. I stepped inside and located the panel of buttons on the right side of the doors. The last time I was here, I used a key. I guess they updated. There was a long narrow slot where I assumed I needed to slip my card, so I did, and the car began to ascend.

Maybe he was pulling me here to feed? Yeah, right. Maybe he was pulling me here to pay him back one of his favors? Maybe he was bored? Oh I had it! He left the remote on the counter and was pulling me to come and give it to him. Wait, did Vampires even watch TV? Cannon was the first Vampire I had ever met. And judging by him, I'd say no.

While humans knew about Vampires, they were not widely discussed. More like an open dirty secret. They outed themselves about forty years or so ago. I had no idea why they decided to out themselves, but they did. I will say, what I do know is that the movies got them all wrong. Like, the whole 'I cannot walk in daylight' thing — yeah, not one hundred percent correct. The more powerful the Vamp, the more sun they can withstand. I heard Cannon could stand outside during high noon.

Their weaknesses? Well, Hollywood got that shit way wrong too. Crosses? I think Cannon wears one. Holy water? Not so much. Blackwood once told me it pisses them off, like getting sprayed in the face would piss anyone off. Garlic? That was just comedy. Silver? I think that's werewolves. *Please help me if there are werewolves.*

The last time I was pulled here, six years ago, Blackwood said he wanted to check on me and school me on Vampires. He told me the things that Hollywood got wrong. But he was vague on what would kill Vampires. After a lot of research, I found that the whole stake through the heart might work, as long as it was made from the trunk of a hundred-year-old Ash tree. The most surefire way to kill a Vamp is to behead them — if you can get close enough to one, that is. These last two points I was not clear on, as Blackwood would never confirm them. Any time information hit the Internet, it would be corrupted the next moment. I was lucky to have the information I did. I still had no idea how they originated. But, I did know turning into one was risky. I heard that only fifteen percent of all people turned wake back up ... raise? And then there's the drinking blood thing. Yeah, that's one hundred percent true.

I shook my head to clear the thoughts. Now was not the time to be remembering what it felt like being bonded to Blackwood. I shivered from the memories. The elevator dinged and the doors slid open to reveal two large, frosted glass doors. I walked right up to them and pounded on them as hard as I could. *Hey, what can I say? I have little tact when my guts are being pulled out of me.*

After a few raps, the large doors swung open. Santa stood staring back at me.

"Lord, child, you are pounding hard enough to wake the dead." Just as I remembered, his voice was flat and toneless.

"Are you kidding? His dead ass better be up! He fucking pulled me here." *Wake the dead, ha!*

"You have absolutely no respect for the Master."

I opened my mouth to give my best pithy retort when a shiver ran down my spine. I visibly shook and could not seem to stop myself. He was close and my bones went to jelly. *Find some fucking starch, Addison.*

"No, she does not." His voice was smooth and deep. It washed over me like ice water. Cannon Blackwood stepped behind Santa and took the door. "I have it, Jonathan. I will see after our guest." Santa turned and walked away without as much as a glance backward. Cannon leaned in close. I could feel his breath heating the skin just below my ear.

"I think he looks like Santa too. That's why I keep him in my employ." Goose flesh grew along all my exposed skin. *Holy crap buckets. Can he read my mind? Oh, please no.*

Cannon gave me a smile with all teeth. A shiver wracked my whole body as I spotted his fangs that were fully extended.

"Come, little pusher. Let us speak." He took my hand and led me past his white room, in which I first met him. The penthouse opened up into a wall of windows overlooking the Atlanta night. I all but ran to the glass. I couldn't help myself; I had to see the view.

The Atlanta skyline all lit up reminded me of what Christmas should have looked like. Twinkling lights. Shining glass. I placed my hands on the cool surface and felt like a child. I was tempted to make a funny face and smoosh my nose against the window. Instead, I closed my eyes and rested my forehead on the cold glass. Maybe someday I could live in a place like this.

I felt chilled hands on the backs of mine. My heart kicked up a notch. Then an ice-cold chest pressed against my back and it kicked up yet another notch. *Stupid hormone-filled reactions.* I was pinned against the glass. I had the Atlanta skyline in front of me and Cannon pressed behind me. I was sure he could feel my pounding heart.

"Addison," His lips brushed my neck, "Your blood is the sweetest blood I have ever had. And, my little pusher, there is so much I want from you."

I tried desperately not to grind my ass back into him. I wasn't getting turned on, was I? No, absolutely not. *Whatever helps you sleep at night, Addison.*

"Cannon …" It was a breath of a sound. He ground himself against me and I felt one of the things he wanted from me. I instinctively pushed back against him, and as soon as I did, I wished I hadn't. Hell, but this man was activating things inside me that should be clamped way the hell down. I somehow found some steel and injected it into my spine. "Cannon, what do you want from me? Why did you pull me here?" He brushed his lips against my neck.

"I want to taste you again, Addison. I want more than that. But, I can tell from your thoughts, that is not what you want. I also am in need of your assistance in a way that will erase a favor."

"You want to taste me? Why?" I was genuinely curious.

He took a breath in, something I knew they only did to seem more human. *Is he smelling me?* I felt his tongue lick the side of my neck. *Sweet hell.* An involuntary shiver wracked my body. I tried to stifle it, but it was useless. The crew had lost communication with the bridge and the ship was going down. His grip on my hands tightened to the point of pain. His body ground even more snugly against me. Places on my body grew damp. Frankly, I really did not want to admit that.

"Because I haven't been able to get the taste of you out of my mouth." Cannon had bound me to him nearly seven years ago. In binding me to him, he had to bite and drain nearly two pints of blood from me. Then I had to take from him a few drops of his blood. He remarked later that drinking from a pusher lent my abilities to him, but only for a short time.

"Just the thought of the sweet ambrosia that is your blood sliding down my throat had me hard for you." His tone was husky with arousal.

My mouth fell open. I mean, what could I say to that? I closed my mouth with a clack. I wouldn't think about the hardness pressing so deliciously against my lower back. I wouldn't. I felt his lips brush the side of my neck and began to shake. I didn't want this. Did I? He had only bitten me once and that memory had not faded in the least.

I opened my mouth to give a protest, but the weak

words were forgotten as his razor-sharp teeth pressed slightly against the tender skin of my neck. His teeth eased into my flesh as though they belonged there. The pain of his bite bloomed and died in the same moment. I didn't know why the bite of a Vampire was so erotic, as Cannon was the only one to have ever bitten me. And his bite went right from my neck to settle low in my belly. He didn't pull on the wound, but I felt his tongue press over the open holes. Every flick of his tongue sent pure heat coursing through my veins. And oh, goodness, I wasn't getting wetter from this. I just wasn't.

"Did I interrupt something?" The voice was sent by the gods, because it acted as the glass of ice water that I needed. I tried to back away, but the hard man behind me gave no ground.

"This isn't finished. And you well know it." Cannon's words were for me alone and they spiked fear into every cell of my body. However, there were a few cells that had clearly lost their minds, because those little bastards were excited at the prospect.

"Lachlan," Cannon proclaimed finally, blessedly letting me go. His tone was so sharp it could slice my exposed skin.

I took a brief second to compose myself. *What just happened?* Had he bitten me without my permission? I would have said no, but my head, which was apparently controlled by my libido, was screaming, "Yes!" Cannon moved so fast. It had to be the speed he absorbed from me. Just that little bit of blood. I was amazed. My amazement was short lived as I saw he had the other man pinned up against the wall. Cannon's arm was against his throat. Without thinking, I used my speed much like he did to try to talk some sense into Cannon.

I didn't have that much experience with Vampires, other than Cannon, that is. I was making the same mistake I made when I was a teen: rushing into a situation without thinking. I put a hand on Cannon's arm. He was just so fast. I didn't see his elbow fly toward my face. His elbow connected with my jaw with an audible crack. The hit caused my lip to split open and begin gushing blood. It was a firm hit, but not too jarring. Nothing I haven't gotten from an overexcited yellow belt. But it was just the thing I needed to remind myself that he was not human, nor would he ever be. This was not a man. He may dress in the suit of a man, but he was a demon. I stared up at the two men. I don't think either of them even noticed what had just happened.

"Cannon. You pulled me here, remember?" explained the new man, identified as Lachlan. He had a slight Scottish burr, but I would bet he had not lived in Scotland in many years.

"Lachlan. I did pull you here. But, that gives you no right over me, nor do you have the right to question my actions. I am Master here and you are loaned to me." Cannon's words seemed to hit the other man's face one by one.

I couldn't see the new man clearly. He was just as tall as Cannon, though he seemed to be slightly bigger in build. Lachlan's hair was shorter than Cannon's and a shade or two lighter. But there was something similar about the two and I couldn't put my finger on it.

"Cannon, I never contested that, but look behind you." At his words Cannon turned and looked down at me. Several expressions ran across his face. Finally, I saw calm and regret settle on his beautiful features. He rushed over to me and knelt down to look me in the eyes.

"Addison, I ..."

"Stop. Just help me up." He placed his hand under my arm; I stiffened at his touch. I wasn't afraid of him, not really. I was just caught off-guard by how he made me feel and how fast it all changed.

"I am painfully sorry, Addison," Cannon muttered softly, reaching out to my face. I flinched. I couldn't help it. I'm a pretty badass chick, but this man was tearing down walls that had been put up to keep him and others like him out. His hand dropped to his side as he turned his back to me in one swift movement. I touched my lip and winced at the pain. It had stopped bleeding, but it was still sore.

"Addison, this brute is Lachlan. My little brother."

My eyes widened at the word *brother*. I had no idea he had a brother. If this was his brother, he had to be a Vampire as well, right? Because Cannon was older than dirt.

Finally, I could see Lachlan in full view. He was just as beautiful as his brother. The only difference was that where Cannon had dark eyes, Lachlan's were ice blue. Where Cannon was a beautifully cut diamond, Lachlan was roughly cut. There was very little polish to the man. His jaw was slightly wider, giving him the look of being older.

I looked between both of them. *Well, isn't this special*. Two beautiful men and me. I must have done something very wrong or very right. I walked over to Lachlan and stuck out my hand to him.

"Hi, I'm Addison." He looked down at me. And I mean that in every sense of the phrase. He looked down at me both, physically and metaphorically. Just that fast, he dismissed me. I narrowed my eyes at him. *What a self-righteous prick*. But before I could open my mouth, he pushed past me.

"If you're quite done playing with your food, maybe you can explain why you pulled me here."

It could have been him calling me food, or even his easy dismissal of my presence, but I exploded. I used every bit of my speed hoping to get him off-guard. I swept his feet out from under him. It was a liquid motion for me. Something I have done hundreds of times before. Like the hulking brute he was, he fell to his back. I jumped on top of him, pinning his arms down with my knees. It was not a position that would hold long, as my strength was in speed, not pure force, but I think I got my point across, as evidenced by the look of shock plastered across his face.

"I am no one's food." I spat the words with as much venom as I could manage. His blue eyes were full of rage and incredulity.

I used my speed and agility to the fullest extent by forward flipping over his head and landing in a squatted position just above him. Lachlan used an impressive amount of speed himself and scrambled to his feet. *But, I'm faster, asshole.* He was incensed. When he snarled at me, I saw the evidence of his rage with a peek of white teeth poking out from under his lip. Rage filled though he may be, he didn't make a move toward me. I looked over to Cannon, who had a wicked smile on his face.

"Lachlan, I wouldn't piss her off too much. She's a pusher. Oh and she's feisty." Lachlan's eyes widened and he seemed to reevaluate me.

"Cannon, as much as I love our little talks, why did you pull me here? I was on a date." Both men blinked at me as though I had sixteen heads. "What?" Like I couldn't go out on a date? I wasn't a nun.

Before Cannon spoke, he cleared his throat. "Please have a seat." He gestured to the bar. The three of us walked over to the black marble-inlaid bar.

"Drink?" Cannon queried.

"Cannon, please." I had had about enough of this bullshit.

"I have a job that needs to be done. I need both of your talents to fulfill this job and keep my name out of it."

This guy had more money than God. He could have anything he wanted. Yet he needed a former druggy and mister personality over there? I was honestly baffled. Apparently, my befuddlement showed on my face because Lachlan smiled at me as though I were a doltish child.

"What do you want us to steal?" Lachlan asked in an easy tone. My eyes widened.

"Steal? How do you know that's what he wants?" My tone was sharper than I intended, but as the song says, my give a damn was busted.

"Because that's what I do, and my dear sweet brother over there would not pull me for anything unless he needed my specific talents."

I had a flash of Cannon and Lachlan at Thanksgiving dinner. Do Vampires pass the turkey and gravy? Or do they pass the blood and clots? I had to stifle a giggle at the mental picture.

"What are you, a professional thief?" I asked, half joking.

"Why yes, actually, I am. And a damn good one." His chest puffed out in pride.

I told Cannon long ago about my sins and I told him I would never do something illegal. I told him I had experienced enough shit in my life and would not add any more to it, despite whatever debt I owed him, though I left out the more heinous parts of my past. I stood up and walked to the door. I made it little more than three steps before Cannon grabbed my arm.

I looked down at his fingers as though they were snakes coiling around me.

"I told you long ago I would not steal or do anything illegal for you. You agreed, Cannon. This has not changed," I stated, trying to yank my arm from his iron grip.

"Addison, do not push me." Cannon gave me a lot of leeway and I used every bit of it. Still, I owed him three favors. Did that mean he owned me? His already tight grip began to clamp down.

"Ouch! Cannon, you're hurting me." His grip didn't let up. He pulled me closer to him and whispered in my ear.

"Do not test me. No matter what I want from you, I will not be made out to look like a fool. I am Master to you, Vampire or not. Do not forget this, Addison." His words were laced with venom. For yet another moment I let myself forget just what he was. I let my guard down and thought of him as human. He wasn't. This man was cruel, and I was wrong before. He did own me. But, I never made a good pet and I knew in that moment I would fight him every chance I got.

He caught my eye and squeezed one more time, then let me go. I wouldn't rub the spot on my arm. I wouldn't show that kind of weakness. But, it would bruise. Cannon's eyes went wide at a spot behind me and he took a step forward. I took a step back, bumping into Lachlan, who had been standing behind me. Without thought I turned around to face him. He put his hands on my shoulders and turned us so his back was to his brother. He winked at me before turning his back to me.

"Come, brother, tell us the score. And let us erase an owed debt."

They seemed to have a wordless conversation, but

hell if I knew what was said. Both seemed unhappy with the outcome. Finally, they seemed to relax infinitesimally. But I would not let my guard down again.

"I need you to steal a drug that is being developed by one of my biggest customers," Cannon announced as though he simply wanted us to go steal a jar of jelly from the store.

"Oh, and you'll have to keep my name out of it," he added.

"Oh, well is that all?" I snapped. I mean really? What the actual fuck?

Cannon gave me his best predatory smile. A shiver ran up my spine at the sight of the white fangs peeking out from under his lip.

"No, have a seat and I'll tell you."

Three

"CRUOR CORP. HAS BECOME ONE OF MY BIGGEST customers. Over the past year they have been buying several of my newest weapons and combat weaponry. It did not sit well with me, as this company did mostly genetic development and research. From what I heard they were the leading company in genetic R&D. It led me to dig a little deeper and get someone to infiltrate the company just to see what they were doing. As if that were not bad enough, there has been an increase in the crime rate lately and the reports are rather disturbing. I have my suspicions that this is all connected, but I do not know how."

"Let me guess, whoever it is, is missing and now we have to go in and figure it all out," Lachlan alleged in a smug-ass tone. He was grating on my nerves.

"Oh no, she's dead. She was one of my bound. I felt her slip from this world."

My mouth hung open. Not only at the admission, but his tone! He said she was dead more of an afterthought. Whatever this so called "drug" was, it had already gotten someone killed. And now he wanted me to go in there and risk my life? *Well, Addison, what choice do you have? He owns you.* Absently, I reached up to rub my arm, but winced right as I touched it. I caught Lachlan's eye and looked away just as fast. But, before I did, I noticed he looked incensed, but I didn't know why.

"What do you know about this drug?" Lachlan asked with an edge to his voice. I wondered what I had missed.

"We know next to nothing other than it's a threat to the Vampires," Cannon replied, eyeing his brother.

"Well that's helpful," I replied sarcastically.

"I know it's not much to go on. But, I will send you all of the notes and files I was able to recover from Phoebe's place."

With that, Lachlan got up and walked toward the door. I took that last sentence as us being dismissed. I walked over to the door, but Cannon stepped in my way.

"Cannon, you will erase one of the favors I owe you for this?" The words were laced with acid and dripped disdain.

I was still pissed at him. Pissed that he made me feel anything, pissed he had so much power over me. I looked down at my swollen red arm. Yeah, I was pissed about that, too.

"Yes," he responded, looking at me as though he were measuring me.

"Then we are done for now. I have things to do," I spat, trying to push past him.

I felt his hand grab the back of my neck. He leaned in close to my ear. I felt his warm breath on my ear and neck.

"Addison, I own you. This could be so pleasant if you want it to be. I am not a monster. But, I do know what I want." He let me go and I walked to the door, fighting the urge to look behind me for fear of the man who was clearly stalking his prey.

I DIDN'T SEE LACHLAN ON MY WAY OUT OF THE ostentatious building. I didn't know if I was happy about that or not. As I left, I wondered how I hadn't realized before they were brothers, even if there were differences. Lachlan was built a little bigger than his brother. They were the same height, but wore it differently. Lachlan was not as refined, whereas Cannon oozed an air of regality. Lachlan's face didn't hold as many sharp angles as Cannon's. Lachlan looked like the type of man who always had a five o'clock shadow and Cannon kept a well-groomed beard. Cannon had long, groomed dark hair and Lachlan has shaggy, light brown hair. But both men had something in common: They were dangerously attractive.

I strolled out of the building, and sitting in front of the entrance was a black motorcycle. Now, I don't mean like a chopper or a Harley, but a crotch rocket. I had no idea what kind of bike this was, but it was all black and straddling it was Lachlan. Suddenly, I had the urge to be a motorcycle in my next life. My cheeks warmed and I looked past him and started walking.

"Hey!" Lachlan called at my back. I really did not want to turn around, so I kept walking as though I hadn't heard him.

"I know you heard me!" he bellowed at my back. *Shit.* I turned around but didn't walk toward him.

"Hi. How may I help you?" I gave him my best *eat shit and die* expression. I really had no reason to dislike him other than for what he was. But, he rubbed me the wrong way. Oh, and he was a thief. He made his money off the misfortune of others. And THAT pissed me off.

"Wow, what a warm retort."

"Look, it's late and I want to go home. I'm sure in the coming days I will have my fill of you. So, if you don't mind, get on with it." I put my hands on my hips and waited.

He smiled and I thought I saw fangs peek out from under his lip.

"Would you like a ride?" he asked, gesturing to his bike.

I laughed. "No. I'm good. I can get home faster myself."

He raised one of his dark eyebrows. "Do you have a car? Because I can assure you this baby is faster." He lovingly stroked the bike. And again I felt the need to be a motorcycle in my next life.

"I have no doubt your bike is faster than my car. But, no, I ran here." His expression said *I'm waiting for the punch line*. I shrugged and turned away.

"Wait. You're serious? You're faster than my bike? That's impossible." I turned to him and walked up, poking a finger in his chest to accentuate my point.

"What part of, I'm. A. Pusher. Do you not understand?" He looked down at my finger poking him in the chest as though he simply could not believe its existence. He leaned in closer, causing my finger to poke him harder.

"Prove it." His words were liquid and slid over my body in a casual caress. I narrowed my eyes at him. Fine, he wanted to play? I was game. I gave him my address.

"If I win," he paused as though he were thinking. I would put money down that said he knew full well what he wanted. "I want to know what you did to be indebted to Cannon."

I sucked in a breath. I tried not to be rattled by the statement but that was *not* a conversation I was having with anyone. Was I faster than his bike? I was like 99% sure that I was.

"Fine, and if I win, I want to know what you did." His eyes widened then crinkled with a slight smile. Seemed like he wasn't too interested in telling his story either. *Well, you and me both, buddy.*

"Deal. You ready?" I nodded. He then placed a black helmet on his head and started his bike. He looked over at me and I nodded, then he raced off. I smiled and crouched to propel myself forward and bolted.

I weaved around the few people who dared take up space on the sidewalk. I blew through streets and intersections. Thank the fates my hair was tied back or it would resemble an abstract work of art. I pushed my speed, pushed myself to the absolute limit of my ability. I made it to the doorstep of my apartment in just less than two minutes.

I put my hands above my head and struggled to catch my breath. I'd never run that rout so fast in my life. Finally, after a small eternity, my heart rate began to slow to a more normal rhythm. I sat down on the stoop and waited for the growl of Lachlan's bike. It took him three additional minutes. He kicked out the stand and pulled his helmet off. He walked over and I looked up to meet his ice-blue eyes.

"I got lost."

I busted out with whoops of laughter. This scruffy man saying he got lost, because he lost to a little girl. It was just too absurd.

"I bet you did," I managed between gasps of air. His brows furrowed at me in disapproval.

"How long did it take you to get here?"

I smiled and stood up. "Just under two minutes."

He smiled and shook his head at me.

"Well, I guess now I know where you live. There is that." He grinned at me. *Shit. I hadn't even thought of that. I need to eradicate my head from my ass.*

"You knew I would win, didn't you?"

"No, I really thought I would win, but I knew I would be getting your address this way," he admitted with what could only be called a sheepish smile.

"Well, I won, so tell me how you came to owe your brother." At this point, I was itching to know.

"Let's go inside before I go into that much detail," Lachlan stated as he walked up to the door.

I raised my eyebrow at him in question but he missed the gesture, or he simply ignored it. *Do I really want him in my home? Could he come in uninvited?* Now, there was a thought. We could test it. I walked to the door and turned the key and walked the breezeway.

This building had four apartments in it. Two on the top floor and two on the bottom. They weren't the nicest, but they were cheap and livable. I lived on the top floor. My door was to the left of the stairs. Mr. and Mrs. Chin shared the top floor with me. They were always cooking something that smelled amazing, which meant I tended to always smell as though I lived in a Chinese restaurant. But, they were nice and stayed out of my business.

Lachlan didn't seem to have an issue getting in the building. I walked up to my apartment and slid the key in the door. Abruptly I turned to face him. "Do I have to invite you in?"

His face lit up with a genuine smile. I had a hard time not smiling back. It was infectious.

"Yes, you do. But, don't worry, little one. I'll make it worth it." His smile turned wicked and my heart did a little flip-flop thing. *Stupid libido*. I narrowed my eyes at him. What was with these men? I mean really.

I opened the door and stepped in and looked behind

me. Lachlan stood there with that damn smile on his face. I put my hands on my hips and stared daggers at him.

"You really can't come in?" I questioned.

In response he walked to the open doorway. He reached out and touched the open space with one finger. Suddenly, orange and white sparks flew from his touch. I squinted at the visual intrusion and stumbled back half of a step at the shock of the sight. It reminded me of the sparks when metal met concrete at a high speed. He pulled his finger back as if it hurt him. Knowing they could not come in my home gave me a sense of comfort I did not have before.

Do I really want to let this one in? Could I rescind an invitation? Is this smart? I paused to think about everything and disappointment flashed across his face. Not just disappointment, but shame. Did he not like what he was? It hurt my heart to see that expression on his face. I gave him a fast smile.

"Please come in," I insisted quickly.

The expressions of shame disappeared, though not before I saw them. Now I had more questions than before. I mentally shook my head, trying to clear some of the hundred questions forming.

My apartment was small. It was a one bedroom, one bath and most of the appliances left a lot to the imagination. My living room held my pride and joy: a huge, wall eclipsing black leather couch. I had to pay six guys at the dojo to help me haul the beast up here. They swore if I ever moved I was on my own. The beast of a couch sat atop a fluffy white shag rug. On the wall opposing the couch was my 42-inch flat screen. On the same wall as the TV was the door leading to my bedroom and bath. My room had one of those built-in beds that flipped up into the wall. When the bed was out of the way, the room was a makeshift dojo. The floors were blue mats and the room also had punching bags, sparring dummies, and some weapons for training. I never brought men here because, well, I was a little strange. Lachlan did a quick survey of my place and his eyes widened when he saw the couch.

"Nice couch," he observed in a smug tone. *Jerk.*

"Don't make fun of my baby. You'll hurt his feelings," I responded, walking over to my tiny kitchen, setting my keys on the small oak table. Lachlan wandered over to the entrance of my bedroom. My heartbeat kicked up a beat as I pictured him not just in my bedroom, but in my bed. I tried desperately to squash that visual image.

"Wow. Where do you sleep?" he asked, poking his head into my room. I squeezed myself past him, grabbing the door to shut it. In doing so I was now pinned chest to chest with Lachlan. My heart kicked up a notch again and I could hear the whooshing of blood pulsing in my ears. Lachlan's eye flicked down to my chest and then back up to my eyes. I was breathing fast and could not seem to slow down, especially when I felt his cool hand brush my arm. I winced as he brushed the place Cannon had injured.

"I am nothing like him," he remarked, about an

inch away from my lips. His breath was warm, yet his touch was cold. It was an odd sensation. Suddenly, his touch became warm, hell, downright hot. Just as the heat he was generating became painful, he moved his hand.

"That better?" he asked as he traced his thumb along my arm, and with that motion I understood. He was right; my arm felt better. He had done something to heal it.

I looked up and met his blue gaze. We stood there not saying anything. He continued to absently trace circles on my arm while I tried to get my heart rate under control.

Finally, I managed to say, "Yes, it is, h-how did you do that?" I couldn't even talk, much less think with him so close to me. His nearness was sending my hormones all haywire.

"I am not like my brother." The thought of Cannon seemed to jolt him and he stepped back, giving me much-needed space to breathe. I sucked in air and made my way over to the couch and sat down.

"Can I get you anything? Would you like a drink?" As soon as the words came out I regretted them. My eyes flew up to his and I was met with a predatory smile. "N-no, I mean not from me, I, oh, shit." Did he really think I was offering my blood? Had I? *Shit.* Open mouth, insert foot.

"Well if you're offering …" he quipped with a knowing smirk.

"No, I was thinking like a water or tea. Wait, do you

even drink, or eat for that matter?" Looking back on it, I don't think I had ever seen Cannon eat or drink. Well, not from a cup or plate, that is.

He raised an eyebrow in question, then let out a sigh and walked over to the beast and sat down.

"No, we cannot eat nor drink anything other than blood. We can sip at things, but other than that, the answer is no. And don't worry, I can't bite you."

"What?! Why not?" The questions flew out of my mouth so fast I didn't have time to control the tone at which they flew. Like a reflex I threw my hands over my mouth in hopes of preventing myself from speaking at all, because clearly my mouth could not be trusted. Wasn't there supposed to be some kind of brain-to-mouth filter? Yeah, clearly I was born without that gem.

His eyebrows again shot up and he smiled. And, oh good lord, it was a devastating smile.

"Because you are bound to Cannon." I looked at him blankly. I didn't get why that meant he could not feed from me. My look of confusion must have shown on my face because he continued. "You really don't know much about Vampires, do you? Well, because you are bound to Cannon that means were I to feed from you, he would know. Knowing Cannon, and from what I saw when I walked in, he would be less than pleased."

"I know he thinks it, but I am not his. He makes me question myself. But, no matter what you walked in on, there is nothing between Cannon and me." My cheeks flamed at the memory.

Lachlan seemed to search my eyes, reading me and

mulling my words over. Hell, he could take an hour to think about my words if it made him happy. I was as sure of my words as I was that I would never touch any type of drug ever again.

"Addison, if Cannon wants you, there's not a whole lot you, me, or anyone can do to stop him."

"Uh, what if I said no?"

"Listen to me very carefully, Addison. Cannon would never take you by force. But he has other means of effective persuasion. Like the things you love." I searched his face to see if there was a hint of deception. There were only the soft angles of his face and the truth behind his piercing blue gaze. I looked away quickly. I did not want him to see how devastated I was knowing my life wasn't my own.

"What did you do to become indebted to Cannon?" I desperately wanted to change the subject. His soft smile faltered. Clearly, this was not a subject he wanted to talk about. I fully understood not wanting to reveal your secrets. It was a type of vulnerability that left you feeling naked and exposed to the elements.

"I got into some trouble a while back. I was blamed for something I did not do. Cannon got me out of the bind. And now I owe him. After this, it will be five more." I could tell by the expression on his face that telling me the details was not something he was interested in. But, I'd had enough of people avoiding things and dodging questions. I narrowed my eyes at him.

"What was it you didn't do?"

"You don't know much about the Vampire society, do you?" I rolled my eyes at the question and shook my head no. This was the second time he asked me this question and I was getting annoyed.

All I really knew was what Cannon saw fit to tell me and what I could dig up. The Vampires only became public forty or so years ago, so there was not a lot of information out there, as they are a secretive group.

"Well, like I said, when someone is bound, human or Vampire, and someone feeds off a bound or tries to cut the bonds, I would feel it. I wouldn't be able to tell who. Just that it happened. Like if I were to feed from you, Cannon would know you were being fed from. But, he would not know by whom or be able to pinpoint your location." He broke eye contact with me and eyed the door. What was he thinking? Did he want to avoid the question so much he could just up and leave? If it were my story with my past would I have done the same? Probably.

"One of my bound humans about forty years ago was murdered. I was blamed for her rape and death." He met my eyes. I kept my face as neutral as possible. Just when I thought I was sitting there with a man I got a painful reminder that he was anything but. I didn't want to push him, so I waited for him to tell me what he wanted me to know.

After a few moments he sighed, "I did sleep with her and I told the police that. But she was drained by another Vampire. I felt her die and could do nothing to stop it. We never found out who did it, either. But I've never stopped hunting him." It wasn't the fact that he said he felt her die or his inability to stop it. It was the fact that he slept with her. The words crashed into me. Had I not been sitting down they would have surely knocked me over. His words hurt, and damn it I didn't know why. I didn't know what to say, so, I didn't say anything. We both sat there for a while before Lachlan finally broke the silence.

"Care to tell me why you owe Cannon?"

I scoffed. But, then I realized I did want to tell him. The thought of telling someone about my past normally sent me into a panic attack. My chest would get tight and I felt like my whole body was being constricted. But, with Lachlan it felt freeing. So, I told him. I didn't tell him about the innumerable amount of homes I was bounced from. I didn't tell him about the beatings by foster parents. I didn't tell him about the disappearance of my brother. And I didn't tell him about the time at my aunt and uncle's house. The house I felt lost in. The house where my innocence was ripped from me.

Instead, I told him about the drugs and the trouble I had gotten into with Reggie seven years ago. A lifetime ago.

"I have never seen Cannon like that. The way I found the two of you. Not with someone who isn't a bound feeder and even that I'm not sure I have seen. That's why I thought you were a feeder."

I met his cool blue gaze and affirmed, "I'm not his. I mean, I know that's what he thinks, but I have no interest in that kind of relationship with him."

He smiled in a way that said, "Oh, you stupid girl." He paused and met my gaze. His was utterly serious and he was unmoving.

"You may not want it, but I would be very careful with him." His voice was unquestionably serious.

"Why do the two of you have different accents?" I questioned, trying to grasp at a different subject.

Lachlan smiled and stood up. "That, little girl, is a conversation for another day. Meet me at this address tomorrow at nine PM. We will meet up with my team and come up with a plan." He walked to the front door and I got up to see him out. It was the polite thing to do, after all. I mean, it wasn't like I was doing it to get an extra-long look at his amazingly shaped ass or anything. He stopped just short of the door and turned with one eyebrow raised in question. The expression on his face looked like he had just caught my hand in the cookie jar. I gave him my best innocent smile and rocked back on my heels.

Lachlan reached out and I thought he was going to touch my face, but he caught a falling curl and tucked it behind my ear. His finger traveled from my ear to the two small scabs on my neck. He rubbed his thumb over the wounds and I felt heat grow from his touch. My heart skipped a beat as it moved to a faster rhythm. The whole time he was healing the wounds he never took his eyes off mine.

This man was not made of stone like his brother. This man had a fire of emotions hiding behind his eyes. I just couldn't decipher what any of them were. I tried to tell my body to calm the hell down, that it was nothing more than a touch. But, my body had a mind of its own.

I knew he could feel how my pulse sped up at his touch. His finger cooled to its normal chilly temperature, yet he left his thumb on my neck, tracing small circles. We both stood there, unmoving. It was like a moment when you're in a crowded room and everyone stops talking at once. And, if someone makes a noise, they ruin the perfect moment. Things low in my belly tightened. As though someone turned the light switch off, he abruptly turned around and opened the door.

As he walked out he called, "I'll see you tomorrow, Addison."

I closed the door and rested my forehead against it. *Christ, these men, Vampires, whatever they are, are going to be the death of me.*

Four

I LOOKED DOWN AT MY PHONE. SIX MISSED CALLS. It should say six avoided calls. It was Kyle. The guy was nice enough, he just wasn't my type. I mean, he should be my type. I should want to be stable with him and Erica. But, all my hormones seemed to care about were two very intense Vampires. My hormones had a rude awakening coming, because that was never going to happen. I really should call Kyle and let him down. I picked up the phone and looked at the time. 8:45 PM. Ugh, I needed to get ready to go and meet Lachlan and his team. I looked at the address and typed it in my phone to see where it was located. I smiled at the phone. Waffle House. Of course.

If there was no traffic in a car I could be there in about twenty minutes. But, I could run there in less than half that time. I threw my hair up in a bun and went in search of clothes. I settled on a white crop top with little capped sleeves. The shirt ended a few inches above my belly button. I paired it with a flowy peach-colored maxi skirt. I slipped on my white lace flats, gathered up the skirt and tied it in a knot just above my knees. I learned early in life that running at the speed I run at means that I could very well get myself tangled up in a skirt, and that caused painful injuries. I could have worn yoga pants and a tank top, but I wanted to look nice meeting these people. It had nothing to do with the fact that I knew Lachlan would be there. That's what I told myself, anyway. I grabbed my small purse and stuffed my phone and keys in it. *Well, Addison, now or never.*

I ran. Running for me is what I would assume flying is for a bird. When I am running I feel like I am setting my soul free. My whole life, I struggled with self-doubt, abuse, fear and self-loathing. But when I run, all of those old emotions and fears melt away into the surroundings. When I run, I feel like I'm in a Van Gogh painting. The colors and surroundings swirl and bleed together, creating this marriage of color and movement. It's a world only I live in. It's a world only I can take part in. It's my place of serene bliss. I never want to stop running. All of my issues were attached to me with a rubber band, and if I stopped, they would hit me even harder than before. When I run, the rest of the world stops. Time doesn't stop really, but for me it slows down. Time becomes my tool, instead of something that rules me.

Foot traffic was a little heavy, so I spent most of my

run dodging people. To them I was nothing more than a stiff breeze as I hurtled past, but any sudden movement could prove to be painful for both them and myself. So I had to take extra caution. It took me longer than I had planned to maneuver, so I was about five minutes late. I paused about twenty feet from the building and untied my skirt, gently patting the wrinkles out to the best of my ability. I took my hair down and let it hang in loose curls to my waist. It was time to get it cut. Running as fast as I do can wreak havoc on my makeup so I tend to not wear anything other than some lip-gloss and mascara. Even with that little bit it helped my sky blue eyes pop.

I walked to the door of the Waffle House, sneaking a quick glance at myself in the black glass on the side of the building. *Guess this will have to do. Why do I even care so much?* It really wasn't like me to care this much.

I walked in and spotted Lachlan and three other people sitting at a corner booth. None of them had spotted me yet. I hated that moment of awkwardness right before you're forced to meet new people. Lachlan sat with what looked to be a dark-skinned African-American man. His head was so shiny the light bounced off of it. The two people with their backs to me could only be described as a relatively large white man and woman with bright red hair. I took a deep breath and tried to shake off all of my self-doubt.

Just as I was walking toward them, Lachlan lifted his head and our eyes met. I still couldn't read the expression on his face, but I did see his eyes dip lower and then meet mine again. *Did he just check me out? No, no he didn't.* His expression looked hungry. *Maybe he did.* My mouth went dry and I tried desperately to swallow the lump that had taken up residence in my throat. The rest of the people at the table were now gawking at me. *Great, freak enters stage right.* The redhead, though, she was glaring at me with a look that was laced with hostility. I reached the table and waved.

"Hi, I'm Addison."

No one said a word for at least thirty seconds. Everyone other than Lachlan looked shocked. I mean, I might have grown a second head but I didn't think I had.

"Oh, Lach, you have got to be kidding me. You brought in a fourth grader to help us?" the redhead spat. Her expression matched the look of hostility I had seen from before. "Look, she's a powder puff. I have jackets that weigh more than her." She picked up an end of a curl that hung down then tossed it aside as though I was simply dismissed.

I don't know if it was her calling me a powder puff or a fourth grader or even her picking up my hair and tossing it aside, but I snapped. Something I belatedly noted I had been doing quite a bit in recent moments.

"What kind of car do you drive?" I asked in a calm tone. I didn't know why but I seemed to have such a short fuse with people recently. I was seething inside, so for me to have managed such a tone was a feat I should be canonized for.

She raised an eyebrow at me and smiled. She really

was strikingly beautiful. Pale skin, full lips, beautiful green eyes. From what I could see she had a body that I'm sure caused a few wet dreams.

"Silver Mercedes." She declared it like she was bragging about her child's spelling test score.

I smiled and bent down to tie my skirt, then set my purse down and put my hair in a fast ponytail. I smiled and winked at her. In a blink I was gone. To her I would be gone for less than a second. I ran out of the building and spotted the silver car right away. This was an expensive car. She had put a lot of money into this car with a number of aftermarket upgrades. One of these was a hood ornament of the Mercedes emblem. With another blink I was standing at the table. They all looked at each other with looks of astonishment and incredulity. I bent down and untied my skirt. When I reached up to take my hair down, I paused to look at red.

"Oh, here, hold this please, I need to take my hair down." I handed the Mercedes ornament to her, then reached up and pulled the ponytail holder out of my hair. They all gaped at the ornament in red's hand. Lachlan looked at me, shaking his head. He got up and leaned close to my ear. My stupid heart rate sped up.

"You may want to sit down before she kills you." Then he did something I had only seen a Vampire do once before. He inhaled a deep breath. Vampires were dead, they didn't breathe. They had no need to do so. So, this action took me a bit off-guard.

I sat down and finally red met my eyes. She was

seething with rage. Lachlan put his hand on her shoulder and she threw it off with a shrug.

"I'm going to kill you," she growled. Her fangs were exposed. I hadn't realized she was a Vampire. In that moment it dawned on me just how much these creatures could blend in with humans. She was incensed. I couldn't help but smile, because I wasn't the least bit scared of her. So, she could seethe and snarl to her heart's content. She could even huff and puff and blow my house down. I still wouldn't be afraid of her. *I have done more damage to myself than anyone could ever do to me. Kill me? Still not as bad as what I have done.* Don't get me wrong, death really wasn't on my to-do list, but fear of what this Vampire could do to me, wasn't either.

"Gen, had you not teased her, you wouldn't be in this situation," Lachlan scolded.

Gen threw her hands on the table and stood up. I would have stood up merely to defend myself if need be, but Lachlan held a hand out to me.

"Gen, outside now." Lachlan's tone was low and controlled. That must have been a warning tone because Gen turned and stalked off.

I eyed the other two men sitting at the booth and asked, "Any other questions?"

Both men exploded with huge guffaws. I couldn't help but smile in return. The slender African-American man wiped tears away from his eyes and slapped my back. *Shit that hurt.* I didn't flinch though.

"Shit, girl, you got a death wish? By the way, I'm

Theo and this fat bastard is Brent."

Theo was model beautiful. His skin was so dark it was nearly black. His lips were the kind that begged to be kissed. His face was made of hard angles and I didn't see a scrap of hair on his face. Brent, however, was fairly large. His belly pushed up against the table in a way that had to be uncomfortable. He had brown hair that grew in what could only be described as patches on his plump face. His brown hair was in desperate need of a wash and cut. But, his smile was warm, and he had charming dimples. I smiled in return.

"Hi, I'm Addison."

"Shit, how fast do you think you were going? Because it was like in the blink of an eye! Maybe we could clock you," Brent babbled, his brown eyes sparkling.

"I don't know…"

"Oh stop, leave the girl alone. No testing on the new recruits," Theo chided Brent.

"Are you both, uh um…?" I trailed off, not wanting to say the V word.

"Vampires? No. Just Genevieve and Lachlan," Theo clarified. I let out a breath that I didn't realize I had been holding. I guess I was simply relieved to not be the only human here.

"So, you're a pusher. Can you do anything else?" Brent asked, looking me over. He lingered a bit on my chest before returning to my eyes. His stare and the way he looked at me was utterly discomfiting.

I looked at the salt shaker. My telekinetic abilities

were shoddy at best. Mainly because I didn't use them nearly enough. For me, running as fast as I did wasn't so much moving quickly, but slowing down the world around me. If I was not careful I would move that quickly most of the time. Telekinesis for me was much the same as my speed. I didn't need to focus on moving the object itself but on changing the world around it.

I focused on the salt shaker. I had to shape the world around the object, because for whatever reason the world was more pliable than the actual object. Weird, I know. The salt shaker flew from its happy home in the metal rack and hurtled past my open hand and hit Lachlan smack in the chest. Lachlan looked from the white dust print on his shirt to me. He did not look amused. I felt my face become flush with heat. I had to bite my bottom lip to keep from laughing. *Oops! I didn't even know he was back there. Dang sneaky Vampires.*

"I can do that. But, not very well," I retorted to Brent.

He clapped his hands like a giddy schoolboy and exclaimed, "Oh, Lachlan. Oh the things we could do with her!"

Lachlan raised his eyebrow at him and did not look amused. Gen walked up and sat down across from me. Her face was lightly flushed. Fury seemed to wash off of her in waves. She really was a stunningly beautiful woman. High cheekbones, a slightly sloping nose, full bowed lips, supermodel tall, and her body could kill someone. *No really, it probably has killed quite a few.* And the fact that she was dressed in tight black leather pants and a shirt that I could clearly see her red bra though did not help me like her in the slightest. I looked at Lachlan eyeing Brent, wondering if he and Gen were a thing. An image of him covered in sweat pushing in to Gen flashed in my mind. I shook my head, violently to try to eradicate the image from my head. *Where the hell had that come from? I don't care if they are a thing. No, really I don't.* Finally, Lachlan pulled up a chair and sat at the end of the table.

"Okay, Addison, I am assuming you know this is Brent and Theo," he said, gesturing to the two men. "This is Gen."

I stuck my arm out, trying my very best to be good, and said, "Hi, Gen, I'm Addison."

She just stared at my outstretched hand as though it might spring to life and do a jig right there on the table. Her brows furrowed and her lips formed a white line. She then looked at Lachlan and remarked, "I can't work with her Lach. She's like My Little Pony."

Oh, well, fuck her. I didn't even know what that meant. My Little Pony? I looked at her and narrowed my eyes.

In a low, controlled tone I said, "Don't pretend to know what I am capable of."

The table went silent. I had no idea if my words had an effect on them and frankly I could give two fucks, but if I was going to be forced to work with them, her, I would not be railroaded. I had to set a precedent or they would walk all over me.

"Look, I get that you don't know me and have no

reason to trust me. But, I don't know y'all either. I am here, so either deal with it or go fucking tell that to Cannon."

Everyone's, other than Lachlan that was, eyes widened at the mention of Cannon's name. I had a feeling Lachlan had not told them my involvement with his brother. It shouldn't matter if I was connected to Cannon or not. They should be human beings.

And there it was, yet another reminder of me expecting them to be something they simply weren't. It was hard to think of them as non-human because they acted like humans. I had to stop forgetting just what they were.

"Look, let's just get this over with so I can move the fuck on."

Lachlan had a look of pure incredulity on his face. Like he simply could not believe that anyone would order him around. I did not want to be anywhere near Gen if I didn't have to.

"Fine. Addison, this is Brent. He is our tech guru. This is Theo; he is our mechanical expert. Gen is good at fitting into just about every space and she was once an architect. And, well, then I am the brains."

For once in my life I kept my mouth shut. I would not touch that with a ten-foot pole. No need to make them hate me even more by insulting their leader. Lachlan explained what little details we had about Cruor Corp. and Cannon's involvement or lack thereof.

"Cannon wants Addison in on this because her abilities as a pusher could prove instrumental in getting whatever this drug is out of their hands." Lachlan lowered his voice when he said the word *pusher*. Though people knew what pushers were, there was a stigma attached to us. Much like with Vampires, we too were a dirty little secret that no one wanted to admit to. Normal, everyday humans were threatened by us. Even though we didn't make up but one percent of the population, people fear what they didn't understand.

"Well, Lach, as much as I would follow you to hell and back, this is a little more unprepared than usual. Even for you," Gen commented tapping her cherry-red fingernails on the table.

"Addison and I need to go collect the files from Cannon's missing leak. I just wanted to be sure you guys knew the situation."

"I'll go with you," Gen announced, all the while Lachlan shaking his head in negation.

"No, my brother is not a fan of unannounced guests."

"Oh? And what is she?" she asked, gesturing to me. Just as I was about to tell her who I was, Lachlan cut me off.

"She is his bound."

For the first time since meeting Gen she looked at me and met my eyes. Her green gaze bore into mine. I didn't let up. Had I, it would have been seen as weakness.

"Fine. I'll try to be nicer. Just keep your hands off my car."

My lips twitched as I tried not to smile. "Fine, don't

call me My Little Pony again."

Her eyes narrowed, then she smiled with all teeth, "Deal."

LACHLAN'S CREW FILED OUT OF THE WAFFLE HOUSE, leaving him and me sitting at the booth. Before Gen left she gave Lachlan a possessive kiss on the cheek and made very sure I saw every moment of it. Aside from wanting to claw her eyeballs out of her skull, I didn't do a damn thing.

"Gen, she's a real sweetheart," I retorted with a smile. Lachlan scoffed.

"She will get better. She's not always like that."

"Good to know." My eyes slipped from the Vampire next to me to the parking lot. It took me a few seconds to register what I was seeing walking toward the building. It wasn't until I saw Erica's skipping form that it hit me. *Oh shit.* It was Kyle. *Fuck my life.*

Five

"Lachlan, listen, a guy I went on a date with and his daughter are about to walk in. Please just don't talk and for God's sake don't mention that I'm a pusher. I really don't want to hurt this guy, but I really don't want to date him either." No sooner did the last words fall from my lips when Kyle and Erica walked in the door. I glanced over to the man blocking me in the booth and he gave me a wicked smile.

Erica was a bubbly kid. She was pretty gifted when it came to Martial Arts. I often wondered if she might be a pusher. When I caught sight of her, I smiled. Erica was about eight years old and had strawberry-blonde hair and the biggest brown eyes I had ever seen. Maybe they would not see us. *Hey, a girl can hope, right?*

Just then, Erica looked over and saw me. She tugged her dad's arm and pointed over. A cold wash cascaded over my body. His eyes went wide at the sight of me. *Shit.*

I pushed Lachlan, hoping he would get the hint to let me out, but he didn't budge.

"Lachlan, please," I muttered in a low tone. Abruptly, he moved out of the booth, causing me to almost fall over. *Real nice, jackass.* I scooted out just in time for Erica to wrap her tiny arms around my waist. I spared a moment to stare daggers at Lachlan.

"Well, hey there!" I said, stumbling backward with the force of her impact. I backed into something hard I knew was Lachlan. He put his large hands on my shoulders to stop me from falling.

"Miss Addison!" Erica exclaimed, staring up at me. She was tall for her age and didn't have to look up too far.

Kyle looked down at me and his disappointment read all over his face. My heart sank. I may not have any interest in this man romantically, but I didn't want to hurt him. What could I say? I knew how this looked.

"Hey, Kyle. I'm sorry I haven't called you back. Life has gotten rather busy."

"It happens," Kyle remarked in a flat tone.

I tried to shrug Lachlan's hands off my shoulders but he didn't move. Erica backed away from me and eyed the big man behind me.

"Erica, Kyle, this is my friend, Lachlan. Lachlan this is Erica, my brightest student and her father, Kyle." My heart felt like it was powered by a fleet of horses galloping a mile a minute. I tried to stress the word *friend.*

Lachlan reached out his hand to shake Kyle's. Kyle eyed his hand and then took it. The two men seemed to size one another up. Kyle may not have known it, but Lachlan could rip him apart before he got out the first word of protest.

Lachlan's hand didn't return to my shoulder, instead grazing down my back, leaving goose flesh in its wake. I shivered at his touch, and when I thought he would stop, he didn't. His actions, thank the fucking fates, were hidden by my body. He continued to run his finger up then down the length of my spine. It took all of my strength not to whirl on him and punch him in the jaw. But, part of me didn't want him to stop. It was a small part — a part that clearly took one too many kicks to the skull.

"Kyle, I thought maybe we could do something this weekend. I mean, if you're up for it." Why was I dragging this out? *I'm such an ass.* Kyle's eye widened at my question. He really thought I was on a date with Lachlan. He looked to Lachlan and then to me. I felt Lachlan's hand on my shoulder tighten when I asked Kyle and then his other hand dipped yet lower as he caressed the top of my ass. *Holy shit, what is he doing? And why aren't I stopping him?* I could feel my body heating from the inside out. Things were clenching low in my belly and my sex was growing damp. I was doing my very best not to get turned on by his touch. But, I apparently had no control when it came to my body and Vampires.

"Sure, I'll give you a call," Kyle said, eyeing Lachlan.

I wanted desperately to get the hell out of there. I think I might have lost the ability to speak because all I could do was stand there while Lachlan's hand roamed my ass and back.

"Well, you, sir, have a lovely date on your hands. Addison and I have to go meet up with my brother and talk about business. I'll make sure she contacts you for that date. She's awful with a phone. She just needs to be poked a bit."

The way he intoned the word "poked" made it sound dirty. I was going to have to kill him. That was all there was to it. I would have to find someone to help me bury his body and I would go to jail. But, it would be worth it.

"Bye, Erica. Bye, Kyle," I mumbled, hugging Erica and moving past them toward the door.

As soon as I got out of the building, I gulped the crisp night air. The day had cooled and felt like ice against my heated skin. I walked over to Lachlan's motorcycle, which was parked on the side of the building, away from any witnesses; I mean, windows. I knew he wasn't far behind me so as soon as I touched the cool metal of the bike I whirled on him.

"What the hell were you trying to pull back there?!" Me yelling at him was almost comical. He was a foot and then some taller than me. But, I was not a child.

He shrugged. "You said you didn't want to date him."

"I also said I did not want to hurt him!" Talk about selective hearing.

"That guy is too much of a pussy for you anyway." I gaped at him. *What the hell does he know?*

"You have known me for thirty whole goddamned seconds. You don't know anything about me. So, cut this shit out!" I was livid. *Why does he care?*

He took a step closer to me, which brought my chest to his stomach. He looked down at me and that's when I saw it. He was pissed off, and seemed to be mad at me. *What the crap does he have to be pissed off at me about?*

"You're right, I don't know you. But, I do know how you will react when I do this ..." He grabbed a fistful of my hair and tilted my face to his, plunging his face down, crushing his lips against mine.

I was caught so off-guard that I froze there with his lips crushing, hell, bruising, mine. As soon as I relaxed, he put his thumb on my chin and forced my mouth open. Nothing about this kiss was really forcing. I didn't want it to stop. *Wait, yes, I do. Shit.* I felt his tongue slip in and out of my mouth, exploring it. I tentatively slipped my tongue in his mouth in return, and felt more than heard his groan. And, oh my word, I could not stop my body from reacting and readying for him. I felt myself soften to him and grow yet wetter. I felt a sharp pain and Lachlan broke the kiss. My vision was a little hazy and it took me a little while for my full sight and brain to return.

"Shit!" Lachlan spat something on the ground.

"What?" I asked, taking huge welcomed gasps of air. This man had kissed me in a way that sent me splintering in a thousand directions. What had he done to me? That was not a normal kiss.

"You cut your lip on my fang. I almost swallowed your blood," he scolded, continuing to spit on the ground.

"Oh," I whispered, reaching up to touch my lip. Did I taste bad? Why had he kissed me? I was so fucking confused.

"Cannon would have known," he explained, meeting my eyes.

"Even with just a drop?" I questioned, sucking my bottom lip in my mouth, tonguing the wound.

"Yes, that's how the binding works."

"Why did you kiss me?" I had to know and could not stop the words from jumping from my lips even if I had wanted to.

"To show you, you need more than Kyle in there," he replied, grabbing his helmet.

"So, what is it that I need, Lachlan?" I really didn't know what I wanted him to say. But I did know that his answer mattered.

His crystal gaze met my sapphire eyes. "More." He handed me a helmet and without thinking, I took it.

"We need to get to Cannon's. I need to get the files and we need to see if he will break his bonds to you."

"What? Why? I mean, why do we want him to break the bonds?" I asked, strapping the helmet on. Did he want to drink from me? Would I let him?

"Just get on. I'll explain when we're there." He kicked the metal beast to life. I quickly tied my hair in a braid and bent down to tie my skirt in a knot.

The whole ride there I had so many questions. I didn't want it to seem like I was yelling them, so I waited. Why had he kissed me? Because I needed more? More what? More complication? He sure added that in spades. It did not help my libido one bit that my arms were wrapped around his waist and I was pressed against his body.

It took us about twenty minutes of dodging cars and weaving in and out of traffic before we pulled up to Cannon's monstrosity of a building. We walked in and went directly to the elevator. I didn't have my ID card so Lachlan had to use his. Lachlan seemed to avoid making any kind of eye contact. Suddenly, he put his hand under my chin and his thumb on my lip. His touch grew warm and I knew he was healing the small cut on my lip. Just as abruptly as he started, he dropped his hand from my face.

"Lachlan, what was that? Back there?" I needed to know.

"I was proving a point. Nothing more." He refused to look at me. Frankly, it pissed me off. I thought about how it felt when he kissed me. Had it really meant nothing to him? Did it mean something to me? I felt a pang of hurt somewhere in my chest.

"I don't get Vampires," I cried, throwing my hands in the air in frustration. Whatever response he would have made was cut off by the opening elevator doors.

PUSH AND PULL

FOR THE FIRST TIME IN, WELL, EVER, CANNON answered his own door. It caught me off-guard seeing him answer, though that's not what stopped me in my tracks. He answered his door in what looked to be a pair of navy-blue workout pants. And nothing else. Clearly, he had been working out; not sure why, as Vampires didn't need to, but who am I to complain, especially right now. Hell, what did the word complain even mean? His body was listed in the dictionary under sin. He had sculpted abs and chest, and a narrow waist, with not a hair to be seen from the neck down. He had the kind of body that begged not only to be touched but to be licked. *Oh sweet mother of little baby Jesus, I can't even...*

It wasn't until I felt Lachlan's warm breath on my ear that I realized that, one, he had spoken, and two, I was unabashedly gawking at Cannon. Guilty as charged! I shook my head and painfully tore my eyes from Cannon's too-exposed body to his eyes. He had an all-too-knowing smirk plastered on his face. *Shit.* I looked over to Lachlan and he looked enraged. What did I do? Sheesh, these men sure were temperamental.

"Cannon, can you go put some clothes on before Addison falls over into a pool of her own drool and drowns in it?" Lachlan scoffed.

"No, I quite like her like this," Cannon observed.

"Sorry, I wasn't expecting you to uh, um, answer the door." Yeah I sounded convincing right? *Just kill me now.*

"Come on, Cannon, let's get this done. I have

places I would rather be," Lachlan growled, practically storming past both Cannon and me.

What was his deal? I shrugged and followed him to the room where I first met Lachlan. He was looking over the Atlanta skyline. I walked up next to him, I noticed Cannon was not in the room so I took the opportunity to ask Lachlan a question that had been bothering me.

"Why are you so mad at me?"

"I'm not mad at you, Addison." He turned to face me. He reached out to touch me but stopped short and his mouth hardened into a white line. He turned back to the window.

"Lachlan, I'm sorry." I didn't really know why I was sorry but maybe, maybe I should be. He whirled to face me, but before he was given the chance to do or say anything, Cannon walked in the room carrying two large file boxes.

"Cannon, I cannot possibly put these on my bike. You'll have to have them sent to my place," Lachlan said, walking toward his brother.

"Will do. But, you could have called to have the files delivered. Why come all the way here?" Yes, very good question. Lachlan glanced back at me and the expression on his face was hard and detached. I didn't know why, but that expression more than all of his others and his words cut me. Had it been a knife it would have drawn ruby drops of blood.

"I want you to cut your bonds with Addison so I can bind her to me." My mouth opened in astonishment.

What? He didn't say anything to me. Shit, he could have said, "Hey, Addison, would that be okay with you?" No, he just made a unilateral decision. Well, damn him.

"No!" Both Cannon and I exclaimed at the same time.

I tossed my hands in the air and bellowed, "You could have asked me. What the hell is with you Vampires? I will get a say in what happens to me." I walked over to Lachlan and poked a finger in his chest. "Look, buddy, you do not get to make decisions for me without at the very least asking me first, if at all." I was incensed. Seriously though, what the flying fuck was wrong with Vampires?

"Lachlan, she's mine. You can do this without binding her," Cannon remarked in such a way that sounded like he was talking about a car or a coffee table.

I whirled to face Cannon directly. It was past time for this conversation, "I'm not yours either. I am not a coffee table! What the hell is wrong with you people?!" I was dumbfounded. Cannon took a step toward me, then stopped.

"Cannon, I need to be able to communicate with her telepathically and if she gets hurt I cannot sense her pain or emotion. I realize we are territorial, I know this. I know it is a lot to ask, but you really need to think about what is best for her. I can't keep her safe otherwise." He didn't even look at me as he spoke.

Cannon, however, did. What could I say? He had a point and I really did not want to admit that out loud. Cannon looked me over from head to toe. His gaze was so possessive it made me shiver. Then his words hit me.

"Wait, communicate telepathically? Why didn't you tell me about that?" I asked, glaring pointedly at Cannon.

"Because I never had the need to tell you. I can read your mind so there was simply no need."

I thought the next two words as loudly as I could, *"FUCK YOU."* Anger flashed over his face and I gave him a saccharin-sweet smile.

"Lachlan, if I do this, you will give her back to me or I will take her back. Brother, I mean this. She is mine. Remember that." There was something on the line here, I just didn't know what it was. My mind slipped to the kiss. And just as fast I thought of a blank piece of paper. I began to mentally doodle on it. Cannon looked to me and then to Lachlan. I prayed to God that he hadn't seen that.

"I will give her back," Lachlan stated in a flat and even tone. He said it with absolutely no feeling. I'm not sure why that hurt as much as it did.

There was a pause. The air was thick with tension and male hormones. I knew they were having a telepathic conversation; oh to be a fly in one of their heads.

"Fine, you make a good point. I will break the bonds tonight. You will need to watch her to be sure she isn't in too much pain. Then bind her tomorrow."

"I'm sorry, pain?" Oh crap. I hated pain.

"Yes, it hurts for a human when a Vampire cuts ties. I want to be sure you're safe when it happens. You'll need time to recover. You may want to call into work tomorrow."

"Shit, how bad is this going to be?" I started to sweat. I really did not like pain. Worse, I always refused any and all pain medications.

I pulled out my cell phone and typed a text in to Darryl, asking him to cover my classes at the dojo. Better to do it while I was thinking about it.

"Okay, so when are we going to do this? And I may need a ride home," I proposed, looking at Lachlan. But, he refused to meet my eyes.

"Addison, it's okay, I'll see you get home. And as for when, now."

I took in a deep breath and tried like hell to calm my nerves, but I was shaking. *Could I be more of a weakling? Christ, Addison, get it together.* Cannon walked over and placed a cool hand on my cheek. I met his nearly black gaze.

"I am so sorry, Addison. I hate to cause you this much pain. I am assuming you will refuse anything to ease the pain?" he asked as his thumb moved back and forth, caressing my jaw. That brief moment of tenderness caused me to stifle a shiver.

"You assume correctly. Cannon, just do it." I just wanted this, the waiting and anticipation, to be over. I needed to know just how bad it would be. My imagination was not helping in the least.

Then I felt him in my mind. It was uncomfortable, an intense pressure. *Well, if this is all, it's not too bad.*

"Relax, you're fighting me." I didn't think I was. I

thought of running, how it made me feel. My eyes slid shut and I slowly let him in.

He broke through my mind like a crystal chandelier plummeting to the earth. The connection I had with Cannon, the one that I had dimly been aware of, was severed; it felt like a part of me was being demolished. I shattered into a thousand pieces. I felt him inside my mind, he was delving into a part of me that I kept locked away, even from myself. I was ripped apart. Not one inch of me was spared. My whole body went still under this painful assault and sweat coated just about every inch of me. No drug human or nonhuman would have touched this pain. This pain was in my soul and I feared I would never be the same from it. I screamed and the world spun wildly out of control then went black.

Six

I DID NOT WAKE UP SLOWLY OR GENTLY. I WOKE up violently. I somehow knew I was back in my apartment and needed to pee badly. Tossing the covers off, I ran to the bathroom. After that was taken care of, the fog that had settled into my brain began to lift. I don't remember how I got here.

I walked out of the bathroom. Shit, I felt I had been run over by a truck. My whole body hurt and my skin felt like it was on fire. I stumbled to my small living room. There sitting on my couch was Lachlan. Why the hell was he here? His eyes roved over me, lips tilting up into a smile.

"I feel like I've been hit by a bus," I rasped. *Have I been stuck in a desert for a month?* I don't know the last time I felt so awful and yet sober.

"Well, you look downright tasty," he said, eyeing me and wiggling his eyebrows up and down. I reached up to my hair. Yeah, it was a giant mess. I looked back at Lachlan, whose gaze had since traveled south. I too scanned my body. There I stood with nothing on but my panties and bra. *Great. Just freaking fantastic.*

I have never been self-conscious. Not when it came to my body. My training kept me pretty fit. And, my insecurities were always based internally not externally. I had a few questions for this Vampire.

I put my hands on my hips and narrowed my eyes at him. "Just why am I nearly nude?"

"Because I knew you would be out for a while and wanted you to be comfortable," he explained, not raising his gaze above my chest. I rolled my eyes and turned around and walked back in the bedroom. Clearly, I needed clothes. I would say that belatedly, I remembered I had a thong on, but I knew the whole time. I found an old pair of sweatpants and set them on the bed, then walked over to the door frame and stuck my head out.

"Hey, how long was I out?"

"A little less than twenty-three hours," he replied, returning his attention to his phone. Twenty-three bleeding hours? *Holy shit.* I walked over to the bathroom and turned the shower on. My teeth were fuzzy and I didn't feel so fresh. Bathing and dental hygiene were my next tasks.

I stood under the hot spray as the conditioner eased the tangles out of my hair. I closed my eyes. My thoughts drifted to Lachlan and that kiss. It seemed as though the kiss meant more to me than it did to him. But, damn, Lachlan was hot one second and cold the next. I didn't know what to make of him. Then there was Cannon. He was the alpha male of all Vampires and he had made it very clear that he thought I was his.

I stayed in until the water ran cold. Which, in this building, was about eleven minutes. I dried off, brushed my teeth and dressed. *Time to face the Vampire, right?* The only clean-ish clothes I had were my old sweats and a white T-shirt I found and oddly didn't recall buying.

Lachlan sat on my beast of a couch like he owned the damn thing. I paused and looked at his arms. I think this was the first time I had seen him without a jacket on. His arms were covered in tattoos. He had full sleeves on both arms.

"I didn't know you had tattoos," I remarked, walking over to him.

"I didn't know you had one either." He eyed me.

"Oh, yeah, I guess you would have seen my koi," I murmured, tracing the artwork on his arms. I had a large black koi fish swimming upstream tattooed on the left side of my rib cage. It was pretty big. And I loved it.

"A black koi fish. Why black?" he asked, looking at the spot where my tattoo would be had I not put a shirt on.

"The black koi symbolizes overcoming obstacles. I got it on my one year of being clean. The koi is swimming upstream because my journey is not yet done," I explained, continuing to trace the intricate designs on his forearm. Someone help me; I wanted to touch him. I wanted to know what made him tick. But, I wouldn't pry.

"How did you get the ink to stay? I mean, you heal so fast. How is it possible?"

"Trade secret. If I told you I'd have to kill you," he muttered in a throaty tone.

"What happened after I passed out?" I changed the subject, pulling my hand from his arm.

He looked from my hand to my eyes. "Cannon had you brought here. I was allowed in because of the invitation from the last time I was here." He smiled and laughed. "That pissed Cannon off. I got you in bed, went back to my place for clothes, and came back here to sleep."

"You slept here? Where?" I glanced around. My place wasn't the safest place for a Vampire to sleep, as it was not safe from the sun, not one hundred percent. Maybe like his brother, the sun wasn't a huge concern.

"Your bed." He had that tone that people used when they thought you had just asked the dumbest question on the planet.

"So, you slept in my bed with me? Wow, just make yourself at home, why don't you?" Who the hell was this guy? He had no limits. *It's called personal space, hello.*

"Well, you do have my shirt on," he replied in challenge. I looked down at the shirt. Damn it. No wonder I didn't remember buying an incredibly large shirt. My brain must be turned completely off.

"Sorry," I stated, turning around to go back and put another shirt on.

"Stop." He got up from his lounging position on the couch and walked over to me. I turned to face him. He had an impassioned gaze.

"Don't take it off. It looks better on you than me." He reached out and ran a hand through my damp hair. "I like the way your hair feels."

I did everything in my power to keep from shivering. Him being this close to me had an unwanted effect. I didn't know if it was him or the fact that he was a Vampire, but he lit every single one of my nerve endings on fire. I swallowed the newly formed lump in my throat.

"So, what now?" It was little more than a rasp and I hated that I couldn't seem to get myself under control enough to speak normally.

I heard him growl softly in the back of his throat. I knew it shouldn't, but that noise seemed to stroke the already burning embers of desire. This man was only adding fuel to my fire.

"Well." His tone was guttural. His muscles bunched under his snug fitting black T-shirt. "Well, I need to call the team and we need to go over the files. And, I need to feed."

At the word feed my heart rate ratcheted up thirteen notches. Would he feed from me? Did he want to? Did I want him to?

"Are you going to bind me to you?" My voice came out stronger this time, despite my fluttering heart and shaking body.

"Yes, but not until tomorrow. I really want to but

it's not a good idea." He looked disappointed. Hell, I felt disappointed and that shocked the hell out of me.

"Why not now?" I looked from his crystal-blue eyes to his mouth and noticed his fangs were distended.

"Addison, I don't think I can trust myself with you." His expression turned to a hunger-filled pain. Sadly, I thought he was right. I didn't think I could trust myself with him either.

"I feel the same way." I was breathing faster. "But, I want you to bind me to you." There, I said it. I stated what I had been feeling for some time. I wished I was bound to him and not Cannon.

"Addison, I can't. Not right now. I need to take this edge off. I haven't eaten in some time so I don't want to be tempted to take it too far." He stepped back from me. What would stop him with someone else? Before I could ask his expression went hard and he turned cold.

"I'll call the team and get them over here. That okay with you?" He was so disconnected. I couldn't understand this complete one-eighty of emotion.

"Sure." I was getting mad. I mean, this guy comes in and completely discombobulated my life and didn't even have the decency to be consistent! I clenched and unclenched my fists. Gracious, but I was frustrated.

"You know what, Lachlan. I don't understand you! You are so hot and cold. I don't know if you hate me or couldn't care less about me." I ripped his shirt off and threw it at him. "Here's your fucking shirt."

I turned and began stomping off to the bedroom. Childish, I know. But, I couldn't stand looking at him and knowing how my body reacted to him. I couldn't stay wanting him to do things to me that I had kept suppressed for years. There I stood in my room. My room that smelled of him. That clean male smell and a scent of Old Spice. I heard the front door open and close. *Good, I'm glad he left. Aren't I?* I found a workout tank top in my closet and tossed it on. I had to get rid of this tension because I was liable to beat him to death the next time I saw him.

I put some water on to boil to make a pack of Ramen. *Dinner of champions.* I then picked up my bedroom and lifted the bed in place on the wall. I pulled my punching dummy to the middle of the room and closed my eyes. After a few moments of centering myself I let loose all of my frustration and anger out in a series of kicks, jabs, and punches. I had no idea how long I spent beating the dummy into submission, but aside from a small break to eat, I didn't stop.

I hurt so terribly. Every bit of my body was on fire. But, I would not stop until I could think about Lachlan objectively and stop thinking about him hormonally. Shit, while we were at it, I needed to toss Cannon in the objectively thinking box as well. I would go from my normal everyday speed to my fastest speed. I was trying to push myself past the brink. This is what took the place of drugs for me. This feeling of pain and accomplishment. This was my new addiction.

"When you're going that fast, I can't even focus on you. You really are something, Addison," Lachlan's voice broke the trance that I was in.

I slowed to a stop and turned to face him. It looked as though he fed. His face seemed a little bit more flushed. That only seemed to piss me off more. Why the hell did this guy seem to have such a profound effect on me?

"When is your crew going to be here?" I asked, trying not to be so pissed off.

"In about an hour."

"Wonderful." I walked into the closet looking for another shirt, settling on a black tank top from the dojo. Walking out of the closet, I ran smack into Lachlan, who was blocking my way. My hands were tangled above my head trying to put my shirt on.

"Shit, Lachlan, did you have to stand right there?" I asked, trying to finagle my shirt on. After three tries I managed to untangle myself and slip the shirt on. Much to my disappointment Lachlan still had not moved out of my way.

"What are you doing, Lachlan? I mean, I am having a hard time understanding you," I questioned, craning my neck to look up at him. I just could not stand much more of this man's hot and cold. I was beginning to think that I was getting whiplash.

There he stood like an unmovable force. After about three minutes of silence he reached to my left and pulled the closet door shut, then slipped his right hand to the back of my head. He clinched my hair in his fist and tilted my head up at him. My heart rate picked up at the sight of him looking at me like I was his next meal. He had such hunger behind that gaze.

Hadn't he just fed? His stare sent a shiver down my back.

He rested the flat of his palm of his left hand on the door just to the right of my head. He brought his face toward mine, and when I thought he was going to kiss me, he rested his forehead to mine. I didn't understand what was going on with this man.

"Lachlan, I…"

My words were cut off by a crushing pressure of his lips on mine. My heart rate spiked and without prompting I opened my mouth, inviting him in. He explored my mouth hungrily; I kissed him back with interest. I felt his fangs descend this time and tried to be careful not to cut myself as he sucked my bottom lip into his mouth, gently nipping at it. Each nip, suck and pull from his mouth sent liquid heat to the junction between my thighs and began to pool there. I was so lost in the feeling of him probing my mouth that I only vaguely recall him cutting my lip. But, this time he sucked it greedily, drinking the few ruby drops in. Oh my, but I needed him to touch me. I knew part of it was whatever was in his bite, but I was going to explode. I pushed our bodies closer together and felt that he was feeling much of what I was. He pushed away and part of me was thankful to get the much-needed air, but part of me to the south was begging for more.

"I don't understand me either," Lachlan admitted, sounding like he had just gargled with rocks. "Addison, you are Cannon's…"

I opened my mouth to protest, but he held up a hand stopping me. I shut my mouth with a clack.

"I know you don't think you are, but you are. I can see why he wants you. I thought it was because I was hungry, but it's not. Addison, I don't mean to confuse you. You belong to Cannon and that is how it has to stay."

I just gaped at him. I mean, what the holy crap? I really didn't know my own feelings other than being painfully turned on. I should not feel as crushed as I did.

"Then why did you kiss me? Another test? Because I am here to tell you, Lachlan, I'm over your little tests." Okay, so I was pissed. I couldn't help it. This was the first time I had ever been kissed so thoroughly and it was causing me to really question my mental state.

"Addison…" he snarled as I darted under his arm. I need air that wasn't tainted with his scent. I needed air that wasn't near him. There was a loud knock at the door. I jumped at the sound but Lachlan didn't seem surprised.

As I walked to the door I called over my shoulder, "Just stop kissing me."

I thought I heard him say, "I'll try." But, I couldn't be sure.

I OPENED MY DOOR TO FIND THEO AND BRENT standing there smiling. Theo held up a long white box that I recognized right away as being a box that held only goodness.

"Before I let you in, was the hot and fresh sign on?"

Theo shot me a dazzlingly white smile. "Oh yeah, baby."

"Okay, I'll marry you, Theo," I proclaimed, not taking my eyes off the box. I stepped aside, gesturing for them to enter.

"Damn, girl, I didn't get the chance to get on one knee!" He laughed as he held the box out to me.

"No need. These will do just fine."

"Can we just pretend to be married and enjoy the after-married bliss?" he asked, winking at me.

"I call best man!" Brent called from the kitchen.

Lachlan walked out of the bedroom carrying one of the large file boxes we obtained from Cannon. He dropped the box to the floor and we all stared at him. He eyed me, then turned to the other two men.

"We have work to do. Let's hold off on any weddings." His tone was clearly annoyed. Good grief, I just couldn't win with this guy.

"Yeah, boss. You eat?" Brent asked, not meeting Lachlan's gaze.

"Yeah, I'm good."

"Hey, where's Gen?" I asked as I realized that her ever-so-sensationally splendid self wasn't here.

"I told her, her time was better spent scoping out Cruor Corp. and the surrounding compound," Lachlan replied, bringing out another box.

I walked over to the kitchen and set the box of donuts down before going to the pantry to grab some coffee. It seemed like it was going to be a long night, so coffee would be one hundred percent needed. After the coffee was set, I went over to the box of donuts and grabbed one, shoving half of it in my mouth at once. If there was ever a weakness for me, it was indeed donuts. I shoved the rest of the sweet confection in my mouth and looked up to see Lachlan staring daggers at me. I finished chewing and wiped my mouth with the back of my hand. Not very ladylike, but whatever.

"What?" I asked, giving Lachlan the same look he was giving me.

"Are you done? I really do not want you to get the files dirty," he remarked, clearly annoyed. I looked over to Brent and Theo, who were sitting on my couch happily eating away. *Oh you have got to be freaking kidding me?!* I pointed to the bedroom and in a low tone murmured, "Now."

I did my best not to, but I still stomped my way to the bedroom. I wasn't some silly little kid, for God's sake. Lachlan walked in behind me and shut the door. I walked over to the punching bag I had set up in the corner of the room and hit it, then slowly turned to face him. *Calm thoughts, Addison.*

"Look, I don't get you. But, if we are going to get this done without me killing you or going to Cannon asking him to kill me, you are going to have to dial down the hostility just a bit. I'm not sure if I pissed in your Cheerios or what, but I'm starting to get irritated."

His chest started shaking and his shoulders soon followed. Was the bastard laughing at me? *Oh, fuck that mess.* I walked over to him and put my finger in his face. I had a point to make and did not want to be laughed at.

"Look, buddy, I have been disrespected, denigrated, and abused my whole life. And only half of that I did to myself. I don't need it from you." My words just fell out. And I could not seem to stop them from flowing. "I deserve your respect. You don't need to like me or even trust me. But, damn it, you will respect me." I was pissed off. I'd had too many people in my life walk all over me, causing me to hate who I was. I thought I was nothing for so long I believed it was fact. I was just now beginning to think they were wrong.

"You're right. You deserve respect," Lachlan agreed, shocking me. I looked up at him to read his face but there was little emotion there. What was there, I couldn't read. He reached down and picked up my arm and ran his thumb over the many track scars I had dotting the creamy flesh. His touch was cool, a welcome relief against my too-warm skin.

"I can try to heal these. They are superficial, so healing them should be easy. It's not a burst appendix or something life threatening," he whispered, examining my arm.

"No, you can't. They run deeper than my flesh. There is nothing superficial about them. And if you could, I wouldn't let you. These are just a reminder of what I strive to never be again," I said, eyeing the scars.

"I don't know why I have a hard time controlling myself around you. But, I will try. And I will try to trust you."

"I will try to trust you, too." I started for the door, stopping when I realized he wasn't letting go of my arm.

In a low whisper I knew he could hear I confessed, "Lachlan, you are really confusing me."

He let go of my arm and stated with resignation, "I know."

The rest of the night was spent going over file after file. After three hours, the words had started to blur.

Cruor Corp. was indeed just as Cannon described. They were what looked to be a company that was steeped in genetics and genetic manipulation. But, they were buying a multitude of military-grade weaponry. And the security firm they contracted out, Branson Security, was one of the best there was. Why would a company who was doing genetic research and development need security and weapons? A lot of the notes were about employees and their habits. One caught my eye as a possible target.

"Hey, I think I have something," I announced, shattering the silence.

The three men looked at me, waiting for me to speak.

"This guy, Jack Tellman. He is the lead geneticist. But, it seems like he is obsessed with pushers. This might be a good place to start. Maybe even a way in."

"Let me see the file." Lachlan held his hand out. I passed it to him.

After about ten minutes of waiting for some response, Lachlan spoke.

"This guy is our best way in. He is highly OCD. He goes to the same bar at the same time every Tuesday. This guy is full of routine. That's in our favor. Brent,

Theo, what have you guys found about this mystery drug?"

"Well, boss, not much," Theo answered.

"Yeah, the notes have two possibilities. A drug that can cure vampirism. Or a drug that creates Vampires. This chick's notes are scattered and hard to read, but that's what I make of it," Brent observed.

"And just when they were getting useful they abruptly ended," Theo stated around a long, drawn-out yawn.

"Let's break for today. The sun will be up soon and we need to get some rest," Lachlan said. He was clearly bothered by the thought of either drug. As was I, honestly. The three men got up and we all started putting the files away.

"Boss, you need a ride?" Theo asked, closing his box.

"Nah, I'm good. I won't burst into flames."

Both Theo and Brent left and I turned to Lachlan. When he didn't move toward the door, I put my hands on my hips.

"Well, I'll see you later, Lachlan," I remarked, hoping he would get the not so subtle hint.

"Addison, I'm staying here," he replied, eyeing my stance.

I threw my arms up in exasperation. "Are you moving in? Shit, man, come on. I have a third-degree black belt in Tang Soo Do, for fuck's sake! I can take care of myself! Not to mention I can move faster than sin."

His resolve was made of stone, as was his stance.

He was completely firm.

"Why do you insist on staying here?" I demanded with a resigned tone. I knew I would not be able to get him out, so I closed the door.

"Because you're no longer bound and I don't want you to be alone until you are bound." It was fact. There was no moving him.

I stormed to the bedroom and walked into the closet, grabbing a pillow and blanket. I walked back out in the living room and shoved them at him.

"You get the couch. And if this becomes a habit, you're paying rent." I walked to my bedroom and waved my hand, telekinetically shutting the door. That was about the only skill I had mastered without breaking the object or myself.

"Goodnight, Addison," I heard Lachlan call out.

I pulled my bed down from the wall. I stripped down to my panties and bra and fell in. I would not think of the Vampire sleeping, slumbering? Did he die? Or sleep? Anyway, I would not think of him. I would not think of his cool touch that inexplicably heated me to my core. I would not think about his tongue inside my mouth and how it felt to have him suck my lips into his mouth. I would not think about the small puncture on my lip, remembering how it felt to have him draw blood from me. I would not think about how incredibly wet I was growing not thinking about him. These were all things I would not think about.

I rolled over and snuggled into the covers, praying like hell that these feelings I was developing would melt away into the darkness. I sank into sleep not thinking about Lachlan.

Seven

I EASED OUT OF MY APARTMENT AROUND 11 AM. And by eased I mean tip-toed like a thief in the night trying to steal a jewel. But, in this case it was my gi top and shoes. That shit should be an Olympic sport. I did not pause to stop and look at the lifeless and unmoving form sprawled on my couch. He did not look just as yummy in sleep as he did in wakefulness, he really didn't. *Keep telling yourself that, sweetheart.*

It was Friday and I had four classes to teach. I really didn't want to miss my classes and needed some away time from the — man? Person? Vampire? — sleeping on my couch. Hell, I did have bills to pay.

I walked down the street to the alley just behind my apartment to where my poor, unused car sat. I only took the damn thing out for work because I wasn't ready to come out to Darryl, my boss, as a pusher just yet. But, I had the sneaking suspicion he already knew.

I didn't know if the parents found out if they would take their kids out of the dojo and did not want to risk it. While people say they don't discriminate, the reality of the situation was very different.

After I was clean, I went to college and earned a degree in business. I went to a job interview and the person interviewing me flat out asked me if I was a pusher, something I knew they were not supposed to ask, and I said yes because I didn't want to lie. And, just like that, the interview was over.

What would have been a five-minute run turned into a thirty-minute drive. Atlanta traffic was enough to drive people to shove an ice pick in their heads just to put themselves out of their misery. Seriously, it's enough to make a nun murderous.

I had two afternoon classes and two evening classes. I taught mostly little kids. Most of my time was spent trying to wrangle cats. But my evening classes were by far my favorite, as both were at an intermediate level. One was for children and one was for adults. My class for the kids was always cute, but the class for the adults was the one I looked forward to, because it gave me the greatest workout.

My day was fairly uneventful. Well, it was until my evening class. I had forgotten this was the class I had Erica in and that surely meant that Kyle would be here. *Ugh, I really do not want to deal with him. Maybe they will skip today.*

I was setting up for my first evening class when I went to check my phone. Sixty-six missed calls and twenty-seven text messages. My eyes widened in alarm. I scrolled through the text messages. Shit, had the world ended? What the hell? All of the texts and the calls were from the same person: Lachlan.

"Where the hell did you go?" Deleted that one.

"Answer…" Deleted that one too.

"I fucking …" Yup, deleted that one too.

This was the theme to the rest of his joyful text messages. His Scottish accent apparently was more pronounced when he was pissed, because other than the expletives, I couldn't understand a single word. Although, when I heard his rolling r's and soft t's, it forced me to picture him in nothing but a kilt. But, surely the plaid would have to fall down past his calves to cover his… *Whoa there filly, calm it down a bit. I was not just having a sexual thought about Lachlan. Oh, but bagpipes… No! Get this shit together, Addison!* I was supposed to be mad. I looked down at the phone and scowled.

Was he really so dumb that he thought that I would sit placidly at home? Clearly he did not know me — or he lived in a world of pure delusion. The texts flashed by and only made me smile. Suddenly, the phone buzzed in my hand. I sighed and accepted the call.

"Hi, honey!" I said brightly.

What followed was a stream of such vitriol that it even made me blush. I think there were words shoved in his anger-filled tirade that were possibly not even words; at least, not in English anyway. He was having a full-on hissy fit.

Finally, he calmed and the line went silent. He didn't need to breathe, being dead and all, but I think I heard a few breaths here and there.

"Lachlan, unlike yourself and your rich-as-hell brother, I have to work to pay the bills. I have two classes left, then I will be there."

"You are not bound. What about that fact do I need to impress upon you? Shit, Addison!" he spat.

"Lachlan, I am a big girl. Trust me, no one could do anything worse to me than what I have already done to myself." It was true. I had done so much to myself both mentally and physically there simply wasn't much anyone else could do that could be worse. He needed to understand that I did not need him or his brother for jack crap.

"Addison, listen. When you were bound to Cannon, that offered you protection that you may not have even known existed. There are more things out there than you know. I am not trying stifle you, but until you are bound I need you to be safe."

"Lachlan, I'm fine." Why did he care? Because Cannon would be irate if something happened to me? Did he seriously just not trust me to the point that he didn't think I could keep myself safe? Every question that ran through my mind just stroked the burning fire that was my irritation and anger.

"Addison ..." I seriously could not listen to his voice for one more moment. I hung up and tossed the phone in my bag. I turned around, forgetting my speed, and smacked into Kyle, who apparently was standing directly behind me.

"Oh my gosh! I'm sorry!"

He put his hands on my shoulders to steady me and smiled down at me. He was an attractive man. But, that's where it ended. There was no heat, no sizzle. I mean, I tried to like him. I should like him. But, even with all of my effort, it still fell flat. Every time I saw him, these feelings and thoughts felt like a revelation all over again.

"Hey, Addison. Good to see you again," he stated, still holding onto my shoulders.

"Hey, Kyle." I said. I looked behind him to his daughter, who was taking off her shoes. I smiled. I loved that kid. When I saw her, I had the urge to be a mother. *Whoa, crazy, dial it back a bit.* I think I wanted so badly to like Kyle because I loved Erica so much.

"Are you free this weekend?" Kyle asked, snapping my attention from Erica and my thoughts.

"Oh, yes. But, not Saturday. Will Sunday work?" I would tell him on the date. I had to tell him. *I am such chicken shit.* I could stand my ground with an angry Vampire, but hurting someone had me a quivering mess.

"Works great. How is your friend? He seemed rather intense," he asked, finally removing his hands. More of my first class began to trickle in.

"Yeah, he's ... an ass," I muttered in a low voice meant for him alone. He smiled and went to sit down in the parent section.

My classes seemed to fly by. I was in the last ten

minutes of my last class for the night when the air seemed to stop moving and grow thick and heavy. *Ugh.* I felt a chill creep up my spine. I looked to the door and saw Cannon walk into my dojo. I froze. What the heck was he doing here? These Vampires were going to cause me to explode or go hide in a well-lit cave. Every eye was on him. They all knew who he was. I bet every single heartbeat in this room kicked up a notch. Cannon walked over to the row of chairs facing the mats and sat down.

I got the attention of the class in front of me and finished the lesson. I walked over to my bag and Darryl, my boss, met me there.

In a low voice he asked, "What is he doing here?"

My chest tightened. How much should I tell him? *Good grief. What a mess.*

"I don't know. I'll go talk to him as I leave." Darryl wasn't a stupid man. He had been a former ranger before opening up the dojo. He respected my privacy, had seen my track marks and likely suspected that I was a pusher among other things, but again he gave me my space. He was more like the father I never had. He was taller than me, not that that was hard, at five foot ten, and thick in every sense of the word. At a glance he may look fat, but I knew if he had the same speed I had, I wouldn't stand a chance. He was Italian both in complexion and attitude.

"Are you in trouble?" He tripped over the word *trouble* as though he didn't want to say it. But, I knew what he was referring to and it hurt. I had never brought trouble here, and the fact that he thought I might be using again hurt my heart.

"No, Darryl. I'll get rid of him." I almost choked with the emotions I was feeling. I knew he saw the hurt flash across my face.

"Okay, peanut," he replied, pulling me into afierce hug.

I threw my top in my bag along with my belt and walked over to the Vampire now standing at the door.

"Cannon, what the hell are you doing here? You cannot just show up here. I am going to lose my job!" I hissed.

"I wanted to walk you out," he proclaimed in a liquid tone. His voice washed over me, lighting my skin to a tingle.

I pushed past him and nearly sprinted to my car.

"What, Cannon?" I demanded, crossing my arms over my chest. He kept walking toward me. He didn't stop until his abdomen was touching my arms. I straightened to my full height, intimidating, I know. He dropped his head until I felt the press of his nose on the top of my head. I felt more than heard him inhale. *Is he smelling me? Why the hell do people keep smelling me?*

"He hasn't bound you yet."

"No." It was a whisper. My full voice was clearly boycotting the situation. I wish my hormones would have done the same.

"You do know I know he's kissed you right? I see his image in your mind. Even now." He pressed himself closer to me, causing me to drop my arms.

"I ..." I really didn't know what to say.

He smiled at me. His fangs had descended and his dark eyes sparkled like polished obsidian. He ran a finger down my cheek, stopping at my neck, then moved yet farther to my collarbone and down to the top of my breast. He ran his finger over the top of the small mound. My breath quickened and my heart might have very well beat out of my chest. His finger traveled down my breasts to my belly button and stopped at my pant line. He slipped the tip of it in and ran it back and forth along the line. He did all of this without breaking his gaze from mine. The heat he was pulling from me seemed to focus and pool between my legs.

"Addison, you are mine. You can fight it. Lachlan can fight it. It won't change. I will have you." His words bit into me. They shook me a bit.

"Cannon, I am my own." The words sounded smoky and distant. His finger still traced the horizontal line along my pants.

"Addison, I kill people for taking what's mine." His finger slipped lower and the movement caused my breath to hitch.

"Please, Cannon. I am not yours. I am not a possession. I ..." His finger dipped a little lower and it brushed the top of the place I was growing more and more desperate for him to touch.

In one smooth motion his hand dipped into my pants and I felt his finger slip into my drenched folds. My breathing grew more rapid and my eyes fluttered nearly closed. He smiled that wicked smile, leaning his head close to mine. He was only inches from me. His hand left my pants and he put his finger in his mouth and sucked. I stopped breathing. I think my heart stopped, too.

He slowly withdrew his finger, then slipped the hand to the back of my neck and angled my face up slightly. Then he kissed me. It was so full of heat it nearly knocked me over. I couldn't help but kiss him back. He would leave me bruised and red from this kiss, a kiss of possession.

I felt a hard length press against my belly. Clearly, it wasn't just me. He flicked my tongue, coaxing it into his mouth, and I followed. He shifted and without warning bit my lower lip. There was no pain, only a deep throb that shot right to my drenched sex. He sucked on the wound, causing yet more heat to surge through me. *Am I on fire? I sure as shit have to be.*

He withdrew from the kiss and looked at me. I felt a drop of blood run down my chin. He swiped it with a finger and put it in his mouth.

"Go have Lachlan heal that," he said as he turned and walked away.

I just stood there. My heart rate had to be coming up on hummingbird-like speeds. I was so confused it hurt. Would it be so bad to be with Cannon? I wanted to slap myself for even entertaining the thought. He thought of me as a possession, like a freaking couch. Then there was Lachlan, and I honestly didn't know what he felt. I sat in my car for a moment to compose myself enough to drive.

"Okay listen, God, gods, Goddess, whatever, can you just please let me get through this night without any more shit? That would be stellar," I groaned, looking up at the roof of my car. I turned the key and started the engine.

I KNEW WALKING TO MY APARTMENT THAT THIS next confrontation wouldn't be easy. *Maybe I will luck out and he'll be gone? Okay, Addison, time to be positive.* I tried to put a smile on my face and walk into the building. The smile, however, was short lived. At the top of the steps I saw the head of someone I really had no interest in seeing.

"Hi, Gen," I called in a flat, clearly annoyed tone. The tall redhead turned to me and looked me up and down. She was dressed in hunter-green leather leggings with knee-high boots, and her top was a black, skin-tight tank top. If she sneezed or coughed I was afraid she might pop a button or bust out. I would seriously kill for a body like hers.

"Oh, it's you." She sounded disgusted she was forced to breathe the same air as me. Well, if she were to breathe, that is.

"Who the hell else would it be? This is my apartment."

"Lachlan told me to drop these files by for him. I was waiting on him to get here." I glanced down to the three or so files she was holding on to. Well, if she weren't smart enough to knock on the door, I wouldn't tell her.

"Okay, well, would you like me to give them to him?"

I saw her grip tighten on the files before she sighed and handed them to me. And by handed I mean she practically threw them in my face. She started down the stairs, but turned to me as I started to the door.

"He won't love you." The words hit me like a slap in the face.

"What?" I turned to her.

"Lachlan. I have known him longer than you have been alive. He has had flings here and there. But, he has never loved anyone other than himself. You're nothing but blood and a possible fuck to him. Don't make more out of it than it is. Don't think you are someone special. The one who will mean more to him." She turned away and started down the stairs.

What could I say after that? If I said I didn't want him anyway, it would make me only sound like a pouting child. I settled on the only thing I could come up with. I looked up at the ceiling and scowled.

"That's how it's gonna be?" I asked in complete resignation.

I walked to my door, opened it, and went in. *Could this day get any worse?* I just wanted a shower, some hot tea, and absolutely no drama. Was that too much to ask for? I glanced over to the form sitting on my couch. Clearly, it was. I sighed and walked over. He radiated outrage and pure hatred. That last one, the hate, caused me to pause. What had I done that caused him to hate me so much?

I was caught so off-guard when he rushed me, slamming me against the nearest wall, that I didn't even see him coming until it was too late. My head pounded against the wall. I prayed it didn't crack the wall. I tasted the sharp metallic taste of blood. I had bitten my damn tongue.

"Lachlan, what the hell…"

"Shut up!" His voice, unlike the emotions wafting off of him like heat waves, was low and calm. It made a shiver run up my spine. Big, angry men have never scared me. I'm so damned fast and have the skills to adequately defend myself, so they really have never posed a threat. But, this Vampire holding me up by the shoulders against the wall scared the shit out of me. He looked at me like he was trying to look through me.

"Don't ever go off like that," he scolded in a low tone.

"Oh, go to work, you mean?" Okay, I was pissed off too. He was not going to control me.

"Goddamn it, Addison! You are not bound! Once you have been bound and then the bonds are cut you become a magnet to all things that go bump in the night." His eyes seemed to become ice. They were so blue they were nearing white.

"I-I-I didn't know that. I'm sorry." It was a whisper. I really hadn't known that. I guess didn't know as much as I thought I did.

His eyes dipped to my mouth and stuck there. Then the bomb detonated. He went incandescent with fury, dropping me so I fell to the floor in a heap. He punched the wall. I covered my head as the plaster and bits of wall fell from his impact. I moved away from him and stood up.

"Look, I'm sorry you're forced to be here. I'm sorry that after seven years of getting my life together I have to be forced into this situation. But, the mood swings and destroying my apartment have to stop. You need to go. I'll call Cannon and tell him I can't work with you and I'll have to make up this favor some other way." I was pissed. I mean, who was this guy? Moreover, I was upset and that damned fact upset me even more.

"You saw Cannon tonight, didn't you?" he asked with his back to me.

"Yes."

"I don't want him touching you." His words were measured, as though he were realizing they were true as he spoke them.

"Lachlan," I said, walking to him and putting a hand on his back, "I don't want him. I don't know what I want, but I do know that right now I want my life back. He just wants to own it."

He turned to me. His eyes were a depth of blue fire that seemed to consume me.

"Lachlan, he did this to show you and me he could. He did it to show you I was his. He said he would kill to keep me."

I looked away at that last admission. I wanted Lachlan, or at least I thought I did. I wanted him over me, beside me, in me; I knew he was fighting to not want me and now I saw why. Cannon would kill Lachlan. My heart sank. In that moment, I hated Cannon. I could never have Lachlan. Even the knowledge that I wanted him scared me. But, knowing it was something I couldn't have, hurt me.

"I need to bind you. But, first…" He trailed off, lifting his thumb to my lip. I felt a warm pulse of power and knew the wound was healed. Tears pricked my eyes. I refused to cry.

"I am doing my best to not want you," Lachlan whispered

My pulse quickened. I just wanted to get him out of my space and out of my life a quickly as possible because this, this push and pull was hurting.

"Let's just do this," I whispered a little breathlessly.

He brought his wrist up to his mouth and bit. Drops of ruby-red blood pooled on his skin. I reached for his arm and pulled it to my mouth. I tried to pull on the wound, but it had already healed. He repeated the process two more times. With each drop of his blood my senses became more aware and hypersensitive. My body felt like it was on fire. I knew with his bite soon to come it would be more pleasurable and intense than anything I had experienced. Everything with this man was more. More than Cannon, just more. By the time I had finished my part, my breathing was heavy and every part of my sexually starved body was bright-eyed and bushy-tailed. When I had done this with Cannon, he bit my wrist. But, when I met Lachlan's gaze I knew he would not do anything like his brother.

He dropped his head to the base of my throat and inhaled. His cool breath was welcome against my super-heated skin. It sent tingles to cover the whole of my body. I tried to stifle a moan, but it seemed to slip out anyway. His right hand snaked behind me and then he rested it on my lower back. He pulled me closer to him and I felt his hard erection against my lower belly.

I sucked in a breath, just as he licked the tender skin at my throat. He tangled his left hand in my hair and pulled my head back, giving him better access to me. I felt him growl against my flesh, sending a wave of goose bumps to cover all of me.

His fangs sliced into me so painfully slowly it made me go weak in the knees. He pulled at the wound, drinking deeply. Each pull sent waves of pleasure down my body that settled between my legs. A most amazing throb began to pulse in the place I most wanted him to touch. He ground himself closer against me. I moaned at the feel of him. I just couldn't help it. Every inch of me was turned on by him, by what he was doing to me.

I wrapped my arms around his waist and slipped a hand in his shirt, digging my nails into his back. He groaned. It was a pained and guttural sound.

He pulled his head back and looked at me. I knew my face was pink with flush, yet pale with loss of blood. He picked me up and walked to my room. My heart was slow, methodical in its rhythm. Normally, it would be wild with how much I wanted him, but now it was just keeping up with the blood loss. He placed me in bed.

"Wait. Stay. I mean … No that's not right." My head was swimming and I felt a little dizzy.

He smoothed the hair from my face and intoned in my head, "I want to. More than you know. But, Cannon doesn't make threats. He makes promises." I was having trouble focusing on him.

"I don't care about me, I don't want him to hurt you." At least that's what I thought he said, but cotton seemed to have been stuffed in my ears while I wasn't looking, so I couldn't be sure. I snuggled deeper into the bed and felt lips brush my neck, or it could have been the beginning of a dream as things faded to black.

O VER THE NEXT FEW WEEKS, I WAS LACKEY TO
Theo. It was Theo's job to teach me how to case
someone. So, for two weeks we tailed Brent. Poor Brent
had no idea we were watching him. Theo called it, "Big
baby watch."

When I asked Theo if Brent would be mad if he
found out we were casing him, he had grumbled and
said something about payback for his house and car
alarms going off at 2 AM. But this was simply practice.
Or that was how Theo put it.

Blessedly, this was our last day watching Brent.
Brent loved five things above all else: masturbating,
World of Warcraft, hacking, his phone, and porn. In
the weeks I have followed Brent, I have watched more
porn than I thought was possible.

Today was my big test. I was to follow him all day
while reporting on everything. Then I was to predict his

nightly activities based on the information we gathered over the past two weeks. I really wanted to pass Theo's test, because I wanted this whole ordeal over with. Lachlan had ceased all communication and that was driving me crazy. On the bright side, I was falling for Theo. Not romantically speaking, but he was the first person I met that never mentioned my size. He treated me with respect. He treated me like an equal. It was seriously a nice change of pace.

Brent started his day with a breakfast of champions, Captain Crunch All Berries. Then he moved on to more important activities. And by important activities, well, I mean the kind that skeeved me out. Thank goodness that didn't last long. Sheesh. His late-morning activities, however, were always interesting.

Brent was charged with getting in with the security company, so he had spent the last two weeks fabricating a resume and credentials to near perfection. It was impressive, really. The things this guy could do with time and a computer had me changing my passwords to all of my accounts. Today he had an interview with the security team's IT department, so he would not be in the tiny apartment long. I had half a mind to call a cleaning crew to decontaminate his garbage can of a home while he was away, but I resisted the temptation, only just.

I followed Brent in my car about five car lengths back. As Theo stated, whilst waggling his eyebrows at me, "Three is fine but longer is better." If I had a grandmother, Brent would surely drive like her. I had this need to do everything quickly. It was in my blood. But I realized that I cannot live life at the speed I would like, so I slow down. Brent moved at the speed of dusty molasses. The man didn't drive, he rolled at an inadequate pace. When he walked, he never did so briskly; it was more of a mosey. The man lived in the slow lane and it drove me batty.

While I was tailing Brent to the security firm's office, I knew Theo would be meeting me there. He was scoping out just what we would be dealing with. And, from what I've heard, it wasn't pretty. I parked across the street from the main entrance to the office and waited. I took the time to write down everything I thought Brent would be doing this evening.

My thoughts kept shifting between Lachlan and Cannon. I needed to find out more about them. I was seriously being pulled between them. I knew there would be nothing that involved my heart with either of them, but I at least had friends of Lachlan I could grill. Just as the idea entered into my head I heard a knock on the passenger-side window. I jumped at the intrusive noise, but quickly noted it was Theo. I clicked the unlock button and he opened the car and sat down.

"Hey, Theo."

"Hey, chickadee, let me see your predictions for this evening, or your boobs." He gave me one of his dazzling smiles.

I smiled back and tossed the file on his lap.

"Sorry. No donuts, no boobs."

"Damn. But, now I know the way to your boobs, er,

I mean heart. Definitely heart." I rolled my eyes at him. He eyed the paperwork with brisk practicality.

"Looks good. Now, to tail him tonight and see if you're correct."

We sat in silence for an interminable amount of time. I took a deep breath. I needed to know if he knew anything about Lachlan. Gen's words rang in my head, *"He won't love you,"* and *"You're nothing but blood and a possible fuck to him. Don't make more out of it than it is."* I tried to not let the words hurt, but dammit they did. They made my chest ache in such a way that it felt like I couldn't get a deep breath. And that simple fact scared the hell out of me.

"Hey, Theo, how long have you been working for Lachlan?" I asked in my best nonchalant tone.

"Now, let me think," he said, rubbing his chin in thought. "I have been bound to him for about fifteen years and working with him for about ten."

I just stared at him, blinking. There was no way. He had to be confused.

"Theo, you can't be more than twenty-five or thirty at the most!" I replied disbelievingly.

"I'm thirty-seven," he replied with a cocky grin.

I was incredulous. "Wow, you look good for your age!"

He gave me a shy smile. "I forget you really don't know much about this world."

I quirked an eyebrow at him, and just as I was about to ask him to expound he continued with, "I haven't aged since I was twenty-three or so."

"I'm sorry, what?" I asked, wide-eyed.

He laughed softly. "I was feeder for Lachlan before I joined his team. I was bound at twenty-two and every time I receive some of his blood, it slows the ageing process. So, I have all but stopped aging. It's give and take, chickadee."

"How does it work? I mean, I was bound to Cannon and now I am bound to Lachlan. Will the amount of blood I have taken done anything?" I was officially intrigued. I couldn't help it! He was freely giving me information without a price.

"First, I can't believe he would willingly break his bonds with you and just hand you to Lachlan. Vampires are extremely territorial and especially over females. And as for your question, it may have slowed you down a few months at most, but you would need to get it at least two times a week for the aging process to fully stop."

"Oh. Gotcha. How, um, does one kill them?" I tried for nonchalant but it just came out as awkward.

He raised a brow at me and asked, "You're not planning anything, are you?"

I shook my head and replied, "No, I just want to know in case."

"Okay, well, beheading them works. Stake through the heart works, as long as it's made from a hundred-year-old Ash tree. And do you know how difficult it is to come by a stake made from a hundred-year-old Ash tree? Stupendously so. Oh, and fire. But if you go with fire it needs to consume all of them. I would go the decapitating route. It's the easiest. With a stake you can be a millimeter off and then your throat would be ripped out. If they are set on fire, they could always do the stop, drop, and roll and, well, then there goes your throat. Most Vampires carry a sword. Though Lachlan most likely hid one of his in your apartment. They are never far from them. Just in case."

My head was whirling from all of this new information. I made a mental note to get more training with a sword.

"Can I ask you a question?" Theo's voice jarred me from my thoughts.

I eyed him warily, then answered, "Sure."

"What's going on with you and Lachlan?"

Wow, wasn't that the million-dollar question.

"Honestly, I have no freaking clue. I mean, the main issue is Cannon and his misconception that I am his. But, I really have no idea where I stand with him. Frankly, I was going to grill you for more information about Lachlan."

Theo laughed. It was that kind of belly laugh that you just can't help but join.

"Addison, girl, you have more than an uphill battle with Lachlan. I have known him for a long time and I have never seen him in a relationship. And in all that time never with a human. I heard he's only ever been with one human. But his situation really prevents him from getting close like that with anyone like that."

"Situation?"

"Yeah, Addison, this isn't my story to tell."

Just as I was going to push him, Brent pushed through the double doors of the building's main entrance. He sauntered out and walked to his car. Then about three minutes later both of our phones buzzed with a mass text from Brent.

It read: "Pending background clearance, I'm in. I have a feeling the background check will get back to them abnormally fast."

"Now I have work to do, but finish watching the fat bastard and report back to me. As long as you do well, you'll be able to start with Tellman."

I nodded and he got out of the car.

Thank God I didn't have classes over at the dojo because I would so be fired at this point. Darryl called me just two weeks ago saying that he was closing down for a few months for renovations. Talk about good luck! Well, luck may not be the correct term, but I really didn't want to think about what other forces were at play.

I moved my attention back to Brent.

"Okay, Brent, let's have a nice, low-key night, shall we?" I asked myself as I pulled onto the road slightly behind him.

I guessed brent would go home, eat, jack off, work on his computer, play his computer games, and jack off yet again. As this was what he did every night. So, to say I was shocked when he left his house around 8 PM would be an understatement. He was even dressed up! Like with a suit and tie. He didn't even dress up like this for the interview.

He all but ran to his car. His hurry caused me to scramble my car into gear. He drove like a maniac, nearly hitting no less than six cars. *What the hell is he doing?* Twenty minutes later I sat outside a small, white stucco house. He preened himself in front of a mirror. After smoothing a few loose hairs on his head down he walked to the door and rang the bell.

My jaw hit the floor when I saw Gen answer. She ushered him in swiftly. As soon as the door shut behind him, I bolted out of the car and raced to a nearby window. Thank goodness it was a cool night and I had worn dark jeans and a long black shirt. I shouldn't stand out too terribly.

I slowly walked around the house, pausing to listen to where I could hear their voices the loudest. The grass was sparse to say the least and it had just rained the night before, so there was mud threatening to suck me down to my knees.

Voices filtered through the window about a foot above me, but there was no way to see them without growing a few inches. Then an idea struck me.

I was telekinetic, right? Well, logic states that it should be possible for me to levitate. I mean, I thought I could really do this. I had a brief vision of me going flying through the window, but shook it off as a miniscule possibility and instead focused on the world around me shifting. I felt myself slowly doing a big bunch of nothing. Damn, I really need to work on this.

Taking a deep breath, I cleared my mind. It took a considerable amount of effort to push Lachlan and Cannon out, but I managed it after a few moments. I opened my eyes to focus on the ground and the house. They were the objects that could change and bend; I was not. A bead of sweat trickled down my hairline. I could do this; I knew I could.

Finally, I felt myself lifting from the sodden earth. I only needed a few inches. The windowsill slowly wobbled past my line of sight. Holding one's own body weight with nothing but the power in one's mind was draining. I could feel myself losing control. I looked over the sill to see Gen feeding from Brent. My mental hold slipped and I fell flat on my front, causing my breath to leave me with a whoosh.

I knew Gen would hear the audible thud I made with my impact to the ground so I scrambled to the front of the house as fast as I could with little breath in my lungs. I looked down to assess the damage. Just about every inch of me was covered in mud. I groaned, then looked up to the sky and scowled. Whatever benevolent being that lived up there was just playing with me.

I heard the window open then close, and made it to about halfway back to the car when I heard a sound that chilled me to my bones. I looked back toward the direction of my car. I would never make it there in time. My feet were caked in mud making my speedy little self, not so speedy.

Then, with a *tisk, tisk, whoosh*, the sprinklers turned

on. *It just rained, who the hell has their sprinklers on?* I was so not cut out for this cat burglar, sneaking around in the dark, stealthy bull shit. Within a few moments I was soaked. I sprinted to my car.

I had nothing in my vehicle for this type of event so I grabbed the only thing I could, fast food napkins. There was movement from the corner of my eye and I saw it was Brent walking to his car. *Well, this has been a gigantic waste of my time. I should be getting paid to do this.*

I waited a few minutes before I pulled out, sincerely hoping he would just go home because I was so over this. But, when I caught up with him he went the opposite direction I thought he would.

I spared a glance to the roof of my car and quickly quipped, "Really? I see how it is."

About twenty minutes later, Brent pulled up to a single-story home. He shambled out of his car and walked to the front door. My visibility wasn't the best, as this was a neighborhood, so I had to park a little ways down from the house he was going to. I had a bad feeling about this. I couldn't shake off the feeling that something wasn't right.

Brent carried an envelope about the size of a folder under his arm. I thought he would knock on the door, but he didn't; he left the envelope on the stoop, all the while looking around him. I shrugged down in the driver's seat. I had a choice to make. I could follow him to finish out the night or I could go see just what files he was leaving.

My curiosity could not be ignored in this case. It was said to kill the cat, right? It wasn't said to kill the pusher. That meant I was safe, right? I sat up in my seat and glanced at the house. I could just barely make out the raised flatness that was the envelope. I moved to open my door when I saw him. Brent was standing outside my car. *Oh crap.* I looked over to see him, hands on hips and scowling down at my door. I did the only thing I could. I smiled and waved as I got out of the car.

"Hi, Brent," I muttered in a shy voice.

"Hi, Brent? Damn it, Addison, what are you doing here?" His plump face was turning a deep shade of red with his temper.

"Ugh, I told Theo you would be pissed. He wanted me to practice following someone so he told me to follow you." I really was sorry about this whole damned thing.

"Now that doesn't surprise me. He's still pissed off I made every alarm with in a square block go off every time he turned his TV on."

I gaped at him, then I couldn't stop myself from laughing. The whole situation was too funny.

"What the hell are you doing here?" I asked between snorts and fits.

"This is my landlord's house. I was paying my rent," he stated a little too quickly.

"Oh," was all I could manage. I couldn't shake the feeling that there was more to this whole thing than I was seeing. But, the reality was I was being paranoid.

"How long?" he demanded with slightly more

composure.

"Two weeks. Today was the last day." I didn't think it was possible for someone to turn purple with rage, but he had somehow managed it.

"I'm going to kill Theo."

"I'm sorry, Brent, he should have told you, but Theo said it wouldn't be authentic if you had known."

He took a deep breath in and held it. Then after a long moment, he released it.

"It's okay, Addison. I'm not mad at you, but would you mind stopping?"

"I'm sorry, Brent." What else could I say? I felt like such an ass.

His eyes lit up as though he had a thought. His eyes darted left to right and back again. His actions honestly discomfited me, causing me to look around with him.

"What?" I asked in a low tone.

"Listen, I'm doing a little side work on someone in the crew. I will tell you about it, but I really need you to give me some space." His voice wavered.

I stood there gaping at him. What the hell was he talking about?

Before I could question him further he announced, "I'm going home. You should do the same." He turned and walked to his car. I stood there trying to grasp what he just told me. I felt like a moron just standing there. I stupidly walked over to my car and got in as he pulled away. He waved and I returned the gesture.

I put the car in drive, but for some reason could

not make myself go. I still had this weird feeling. I glanced over to the door where the envelope … was no longer laying. In the time that it took Brent and me to talk, someone had opened the door and retrieved the envelope. And I never heard a moment of it.

I couldn't make heads or tails of any of this, but I did know one thing. Something about this house and Brent did not sit well with me. And the feeling Brent was on to something about someone I knew made me question everyone.

For the life of me, I felt like I was being watched. I eased the car out of park and slowly drove past the house. It wasn't until I was no less than two miles away did the feeling of slimy dread ease. But, whatever had been in that house had left its mark, because I would always be looking over my shoulder.

Nine

THE NEXT TWO MONTHS, AFTER BRENT, WERE spent casing and tailing my target. Lachlan only sent me text messages. He still refused to see me or talk to me. It really was for the best, yet I couldn't help but be hurt by it. I tried to ditch Kyle to the best of my ability, but he was going to take a firmer hand and more concentration than I could muster at the moment. For now, at least I was successful at dodging him.

My target was Jack Tellman. Unlike my practice subject, this guy was OCD to the extreme. He had his life so scheduled that he only took a piss or shit at certain times a day. Oh, God forbid the urge hit him in an inopportune time, the man held it! Talk about discipline; I should take a lesson. And he did not vary so much as five minutes from any scheduled appointment, ever.

Every day at 6:45 AM Jack arrived at work. He

always used the entrance in the front of the main building, even though the lab was located on the third sublevel of a smaller building. This wasn't just a company, for crap's sake, it was a compound. The place even had its own Starbucks.

The buildings were surely linked via underground tunnels of some kind. At least that was what Brent said, as he'd been monitoring the cameras for more than two months.

Jack, with his OCD tendencies, was constantly aware of his surroundings, so being close to him was out of the question. The guy was a freaking machine. Lunch every day was at the stroke of noon. He walked over to Chipotle every day and had the same damn burrito. After lunch, he went to the bathroom on the second floor of the main building and then returned to work. He used that bathroom because it was located near his office. Or, that was what I surmised. He was the only lab worker to have his office in the main building. He exited the buildings every day at 6:45 PM, except Tuesdays and Thursdays. On those days he left at 9 PM and went directly to Fat Fred's Bar. He ate dinner, talked to no one, drank one glass of red wine, still talked to no one, and then went to his home in Vinings.

He was often approached by women and shot each one down with a few words. He was a good-looking man. His body was lean, but not scrawny. He reminded me of Zachary Quinto, with dark, distinguished eyebrows and a strong jaw that curved into a square chin. Other than the hair on his head and his eyebrows, the man didn't have so much as a five o'clock shadow. It was impressive, really. He stood about six foot even with chocolate-brown hair. On the days he didn't stay late, he went home and didn't leave again until the next morning. His weekends were full of wild sex parties and … okay, yeah, no. The only time this guy left was to go grocery shopping on Saturdays and one Sunday a month he went to get a haircut. He seemed to be working from home, but it was hard to get a good look, as his security was way higher and tighter than Fort damn Knox.

By month two of watching this guy, I knew his schedule so well I could have been him. Well, I wasn't as tall or male, but good grief he was predictable. I could not take much more of this guy. The dojo had been opened from renovations a few weeks ago and I was missing a lot of work. I really couldn't afford to lose my job. I was living on savings for the time being, but something had to give and soon.

I dialed Lachlan's number and, like always, he didn't answer.

His voicemail message stated, "Speak."

"Lachlan, I really think I have the information I need to move in on this guy. I am about to pull my hair out watching him. Call me back; we need to talk!" *Oh, and you're an insufferable dick.* I didn't say that last bit, but oh how I wanted to.

And speaking of predictable. My phone buzzed with a text message.

"Do not approach him. You're not ready."

I had already talked to Theo and Brent and they had no idea why Lachlan was being so cautious. *I'm not ready? What the hell does that mean?* I have spent two freaking months tailing a guy as predictable as the sun. I was losing money. I was losing time. I was losing my mind! Something had to give. I mean, what harm would approaching this guy cause? If he really wanted me to be helpful, it was time I get off my ass and put myself into the situation. I was so done sitting out just waiting for Lachlan to tell me I was "ready," whatever that meant.

I got the green light from Theo to watch this guy. What more did I need to know? I could set my watch by this guy.

I looked at the time on my phone, 8:07 PM. It was Tuesday, so he would be at Fat Frank's at in about an hour and a half. I had enough time to shower, dry my hair, dress, and practice just how I would spark his interest in me. Before hopping in the shower I shot Theo a text.

"Be at my place at 9. Don't tell Lachlan."

I showered with quick efficiency and started drying my hair. I needed to look enticing, so I left my hair down and kept its natural soft curl. At this point, my hair hung almost to my waist. I glanced at my phone and saw a missed text from Theo.

"Are we doing something naughty? If so, I'm in."

I smiled down at my phone and typed in, "Of course. Bring handcuffs ;)"

I set the phone down and started putting my makeup on. I used a smoky eye with hints of blue. I put some lip-gloss on and looked at myself in the mirror. I hardly recognized myself. Like most women, I have never thought of myself as beautiful, but right now I thought I looked pretty damn good. Right as I had the thought, I felt ashamed. Like having the thought that I was indeed beautiful made me shallow or vain. I shook my head. It's a shame that women can't admire themselves and not feel ashamed for doing so. I made a mental note to talk about this with my students.

I walked out to eye the dress I picked out just for this occasion. It was an all-lace dress, sleeveless and short. Like "I better not bend over too far" short. As much as I loved short-sleeved things, putting makeup on my arms did get old. Hanging from the bottom of the dress was scalloped lace edges. And the color was royal blue. I chose blue because my already blue eyes seemed to stand out even more.

I slipped on the dress and zipped it up most of the way. I could never manage to zip any dress up all the way without help. I grabbed my silver high heels just as I heard a knock at the door.

"Come in!" I yelled.

"Hey, girl," Theo's even voice called through my apartment.

I walked out of the bedroom holding my killer heels and Theo's eyes went wide at the sight of me.

"Whoa! Let me look at you!" he said, walking over and lifting my right hand above my head. I spun around.

He let out a loud whistle and my cheeks warmed with flush.

"Damn, I knew I should have brought the handcuffs!" He looked me up and down.

"Well, how about you finish zipping me up and I'll let you in on my plan."

He zipped me up and I told him my plan. He looked to be a mix of horrified and intrigued. He rubbed his chin and went silent for a long time after I finished speaking.

"Well?" I asked impatiently. I knew we had little time to cogitate on this. I would do this alone, but I really wanted some kind of back up.

"Addison, Lachlan will kill us." My heart sank at his words. I hadn't realized just how much I wanted Theo to be there.

"Okay, I don't want you to get in trouble with him." I couldn't help but feel a bit dejected.

"Oh, I didn't say I wouldn't do it, but be ready for him to kill us. I'm with you, it's time to move on this." I met his dark gaze and his eyes sparked with defiance. I smiled. Hook, line, and sinker.

"Let's do this."

Fat Frank's Bar was set into a row of brick-faced shops that ran along the city block. Parking was nonexistent. The signs in the windows of Frank's boasted that they had the best selection for craft beer and best bar food this side of the Mason-Dixon Line.

Good to know.

My heart was hammering against my chest. I placed a hand just over the pounding and closed my eyes. I needed to calm the heck down or I would blow this. I spent all of my extra hours these past two month perfecting how I would out myself to him. I was getting substantially better at using my telekinetic ability. But, what if something went wrong? I opened my eyes to find Theo observing me.

"You okay, babe?" He looked genuinely concerned. I have never had someone worry about my well-being and it warmed me.

"Yeah, just nervous," I said, letting out a breath I didn't realize I held.

"Don't be. Think about it like a date. And you look smokin'. I don't think you'll have any issues."

I looked past Theo into the bar. All I could see were the bright yellow lights spilling out of the lightly frosted windows. I knew he was in there. I knew he was ordering a glass of red wine and about to order his pot roast dinner. I knew what he was doing. I snuck into the bar one night while he was there and was able to observe him without his notice. I was ready for this, despite what Lachlan thought. *Time to inject a little starch into your spine, Addison.* I took a deep breath and exited the car.

Frank's on the outside looked like just another bar. But, when I stepped in I was transported to another time. The bar was made out of darkest mahogany and the accents were all gold, with crystal chandeliers and white-marbled floors. It reminded me of something straight out of *The Great Gatsby*. I walked in and wasn't greeted by anyone, so I headed over to the bar, spotting Jack right away. He was slowly sipping his wine, rolling the liquid over his tongue and truly tasting it in the way people who knew how to taste wine did. I walked over to him. *Now or never.*

"May I?" I asked in a soft voice. He looked over at me and gave me a quick once over, then nodded and returned to his wine. However, he did sneak a few glances at me.

The bartender came over and placed a white napkin in front of me and questioned, "What can I get ya?"

"Oh, I don't know. I like wine. Um, sir, do you know much about wine?" I asked, hoping Jack would get the hint. He did and eyed me.

"Red or white?" he asked in a bored tone.

"Red."

"Fred, get her a glass of the merlot," he ordered, never making eye contact with me.

Fred went to retrieve the wine. Only moments later I had a glass of red wine sitting in front of me. I moved the glass to my right and swiveled in my chair to angle myself just right, facing Jack.

"Thank you for the recommendation," I said, scooting off the stool. I turned too quickly and caught the glass of wine with my hand, sending the glass careening to the floor. I threw my hands out and used my telekinetic ability to stop the glass and wine from falling to the ground. Bending down, I picked the levitating glass up and scooped all of the wine that floated in crimson orbs. I released my mental hold on the orbs and they splashed into the glass. The whole thing only took about ten seconds but I knew Jack saw every moment. I had sweat rolling down my spine from the mental strain of holding both the glass and the wine. I worked for two months to perfect this, but damn it took a lot out of me.

Pretending to be embarrassed, I exclaimed, "Oh my goodness. I am so sorry!" I had never outed myself in such a way, so the mortification that followed was easy to fake, as it wasn't fake.

I set the wine glass on the bar and met Jack's green eyes, which sparked with interest and lust. *Lust? My, my Mr. Jack, you do love pushers, don't you?* I tried my best to stifle a shiver of disgust.

"I need to go," I proclaimed, slapping a twenty on the counter. I ran out of the bar, standing on the sidewalk and acting as though I was waiting on a ride. And just like I knew he would, Jack came running out of the bar.

"Hey!" he called.

I turned my back to him and stated, "Look, whatever mean thing you're going to say about pushers, save it. I don't want to hear it."

I felt his hand on my shoulder as he pleaded, "Wait, please. I'm not like that. I just want to, I don't know, get to know you. God, that sounds so desperate. It's just it's not every day I see someone so beautiful and intriguing." His tone was smug, which threw me off-guard.

I turned and looked up at him. "You're the first person who didn't care I was a pusher."

He smiled. He put his hands in his pockets and rocked back on his heels.

"It doesn't matter to me. Please join me for dinner." His gaze was hungry as it swept over me.

I smiled and said sweetly, "You know what? I think I will."

THE NEXT TWO HOURS WERE SPENT LISTENING TO Jack talk about his job and how he loved all things genetic and then about me and my genetics. I tried my best to be interested, but good freaking grief this guy was going to bore me to death. However, his eyes lit up with passion when he spoke about his job and that was slightly endearing. Despite how much he loved his job, I had a bad feeling about him I just could not shake. It was like he was putting on just as much of an act as I was. I shook my head to clear it of the strange alarm bells going off.

"Did you know there are geneticists out there right now looking to isolate the pusher gene to see if they can develop a cure for it?" he asked around a bite of ice cream.

I froze. A cure? Why? I would never want to get rid of my abilities. I was honestly horrified that there was a study that would end in some kind of cure for pushers. We didn't need to be cured.

"Do you think we need a cure?" I asked, trying to mask the indignation I was feeling.

He looked at me, obviously trying to read me. I made a mental note to play poker with this guy; I would seriously make bank.

"I think people who would like to be normal should get that chance."

"And you don't think the government, who by the way has been so caring and open to pushers, would force this potential vaccine on us? Or any of the other four thousand hate groups out there?" My tone was seriously getting harsh. I couldn't help it.

He reached over to me and put his warm hand over mine and cooed, "I do think they would. I am not so naive to think they would have pure intentions. But, I think pushers have enough support that they would be met with a lot of resistance." He looked like he believed in what he said. There was something I couldn't place though.

I had to change the subject or I would really turn this guy off.

"So, Jack, what are you working on now?"

"Fruit. I am genetically manipulating fruit. Trying to create seeds that grow in tropical climates to grow in different types of places. All in hopes of getting people in third world nations more food," he stated with such clinical detachment that I knew it was a lie. This guy could not lie to save his life.

"How noble of you." I gave him a shy smile.

"Well, I am working on a side project you might

think is interesting. In fact, I would love to tell you more about it, but I would need to show you," he confessed, hinting at more.

My heart rate picked up at the thought of finding out just what this asshole was up to. I was trying to decide if I should go with him or not when a tingle went up my spine as I heard a voice in my head. The voice was full of so much rage I had a hard time not shaking my head in pain.

"Addison! I cannot fucking believe you." The voice kept yelling in my head. Followed by several growls and snarls. It was Lachlan. *Shit! How the crap had he found out?*

I answered back with, "Hi, honey, I can't talk right now but please leave a message at the beep ..." I couldn't help it! Apparently my mental voice had less of a filter than my physical one. And that wasn't saying much.

"Well?" Jack questioned, staring at me blankly.

Shit! What had he said? "I'm sorry! What?" I knew he was going to think I'm a space cadet, but right now with an angry Vampire yelling in my head I was doing my best not to explode.

He laughed low in his chest and asked, "I know this is soon, but would you like to come to my place?"

My heart pounded with anticipation. This could be the break we needed to get Lachlan and Cannon off my back. This wasn't the plan, but Theo could adjust.

"Sure. I have a car I can drive."

He got up and offered his hand to me. I took it and he pulled me up, standing so close I wanted to take a few steps back. I felt his arm snake around my waist, essentially trapping me against him. He lifted my hand to his mouth and placed a warm kiss against my knuckles. This didn't send warmth through me like when Lachlan kissed me or even sensual heat like with Cannon. This was all icky and sticky. It gave me the willies and I had to stifle a shiver. Even just that brief of a kiss reminded me of how it felt to have a spider crawl over your hand when you weren't paying attention. Still, I gave him my best smile, but I knew it was tight. This guy was a bit unnerving. There was no real reason for me to feel that way, but I did.

We walked out of the bar and he gave me directions to his house.

Heading to my car, I found Lachlan sitting in it, looking back to see if Jack was there. He had already gone. I could feel the anger and incredulity wafting off of Lachlan in heat waves. I was not going to let him bully or intimidate me. *Yeah, whatever helps you sleep at night.*

I opened the driver's side door and sat down.

"Where's Theo?" I asked, not meeting his eyes.

"I sent him home. Now, you want to tell me what the fuck you're doing?" He was seething. His words were like a slap against my skin. I glanced over to see him looking at the exposed skin of my thighs.

"I-I was sick of you not trusting me. But, I don't have time for this. He invited me to his house. And I'm going," I declared, buckling my seatbelt and pulling away from the curb.

"The hell you are. This is not how I run things. Pull over, Addison." If a person could be boiling, he would be.

"No."

He slammed his fists down on the dashboard and snarled, "goddamn it, Addison!" I tried not to flinch, but still jumped at the audible intrusion. And, damn it, that crack I heard better have been his bones, not my dash!

We sat in silence the rest of the way to Jack's house. The house was all brick and had an old-world feel, but the most prominent thing about it was that it was fucking massive. Why did he need all of that space? He was one person! I didn't get it, but I guess I didn't need to. Though there were two large oak trees in the front yard, there was not a single leaf on the ground and the lawn was manicured within an inch of its life.

Just as I got out of the car, Lachlan grabbed my wrist. I looked at him and saw that he wasn't just mad, he was hurt. Anger and him being pissed I could deal with, but the hurt, that stung.

"I am beyond pissed with you. But, it's too late now. Take this and slip it in his drink. It won't take long and he should be out like a light. I will be here. Call to me mentally if you need help," he said as he placed a small pill in my hand. I promptly put the pill in my bra and his eyebrows raised in question.

"I don't have pockets." I got out of the car and walked to the door and knocked.

"Addy! Glad to see you. Please come in." I winced at his use of the name I had given him. My thoughts slid to the only person to use that name. Aaron, my brother.

"Hi, Jack! This place is beautiful!" I exclaimed, trying to push all other thoughts aside. The door was solid carved oak, with ornate twists and curls carved into the wood. It probably took months just to make the door. Maybe I should become a geneticist because clearly they made bank.

He placed a hand at my back and responded, "Thank you. Let me show you around."

The entry was made of oak. In fact, there was so much oak in this house it lent everything an amber glow, enhancing the dark-blue accents along with brass fixtures everywhere. I didn't know if it was the amber hue or the wood, but the house felt so warm. As Jack led me through the house his demeanor became more impatient and less kind. His hand at my lower back became more forced.

"So, what is this other project?" I asked as he led me to yet another guest bedroom.

"Well, I must admit there are a few reasons I wanted you to come over here," he replied, pausing in the hallway. We were still on the ground floor of the house and just beyond us was what looked to be a kitchen with the amount of light that was spilling into the hallway.

As we rounded the corner I noticed that to the right there was an informal living room, and to the left there was, indeed, a kitchen. I turned to Jack and give him a sweet innocent smile.

"Oh? And what are those?" I asked, pushing the flirt into my voice.

He stepped closer to me and brushed a hand over my cheek. His gaze was full of lust and something else I couldn't name.

"First, I want to do this…" He let his words fall off and his lips pick up where they left off. He kissed me. I wasn't expecting it, so for a second I stood there dumbfounded. Then, remembering why I was there, I kissed him back. It wasn't unenjoyable; it just felt wrong.

His other hand crept up my side and he cupped my breast. I broke the kiss and sucked in a breath, pushing his arm gently down. His face flashed with rage. I took a step back and tried to give him a sweet grin.

"Whoa there, killer! Not going to offer a lady a drink?" I asked sweetly.

"Where are my manners?" Jack questioned, turning and walking to the kitchen. I had been counting my drinks since the bar and knew I had two drinks there. But, I counted four for him, so he should be well on his way to sloshed.

"So, what else did you want to show me? What are you working on?" I asked as I walked over to the maroon plush couch. It had nothing on the beast, but it was okay, if you liked that kind of thing. Just before I sat down, I reached into my bra and pulled out the small pill that Lachlan gave me. I held it in my left hand, waiting to use it. I was having a hard time getting my erratic heartbeat to calm down.

He walked over with two glasses of red wine.

"Well, I was wondering if I could get a few drops of blood from you," he said as though he were asking to borrow a library book.

"Um … What are you going to do with it?" I asked hesitantly.

"Well, I have this project I have been working on. You know how the Vampires are selective about who they turn? Like they won't turn a pusher?"

"Yeah?" I tried my best to mask my excitement. It was hard to hear him with the increased blood flow from my pumping heart. The whooshing in my ears was nearly drowning every word. But, what I heard next was clear as a bell.

"Well, we are turning our own pushers into Vampires," he stated, obviously proud of himself. I had no idea what to say. My mouth was just hanging open. I had expected it to be big, whatever it was, but not this. I realized his eyes weren't quite focusing on me and his words were a little slurred. Seemed as though his wine was beginning to hit him.

"H-h-how are you doing that? I mean, wow," was all I could manage. My mouth was dry and my throat was tight. I reached over and grabbed the two wines from the small table he sat them on. In the process I dropped the pill in his, then handed the glass to him. We both took a slow sip. He smiled as he brought the glass from his lips. *Shit, can he taste it? Does he know?* Apparently the paranoia had fully set in as just about every possibility entered into my head at once.

He took another long pull from his glass and, once finished, he set the glass down and scooted closer to me. He moved aside my hair and dipped his face to my ear and whispered, "That, Addy, is a secret." I felt his hand caress the nape of my neck. He then moved down to my collar bone.

"What about the blood sample?" I asked, a little breathless. Not from being aroused, but from simply not wanting him near me.

"That too." He shifted yet closer to me. He kissed my neck and it felt like tiny spiders covering my body. He slowly turned my face to his and kissed me. It was slow and filled with his lust, but it wasn't insistent. Thank God.

I pulled away and broke the kiss, pretending to be breathless. "Maybe before things go further, you should take that sample. Wouldn't want to forget."

"You're right! Then we can get back to other activities," he said, getting up and offering me a hand. I was having a hard time gauging this guy, as he was being way more aggressive than he was at the bar. I was starting to get a weird feeling. Like Deja-vu or maybe a foreboding. Maybe it was just that he was drunk? I shook my head to try to clear it and focus on what was happening.

I grabbed his wine for him and left mine. Just what I needed was to pass out in a drugged stupor, because that was something I would do. He walked into one of the guest rooms. This room had a huge assortment of swords, daggers, and other weaponry on the wall and they all looked to be authentic. I walked over to study a sword that seemed to be the center of his collection. It was black from hilt to tip, encased in glass and mounted to the center of his collection. Clearly the crowning jewel. This was no foil or saber. The sheath looked to have a normal hilt and then it tapered out in a football shape and narrowed into a metal tip. The sword itself was just above the scabbard. The blade looked to be double edged and about a yard long. The sheath looked nothing like the blade. I wondered why the blade was not kept in its sheath, but I was not an authority on sword care. And this one looked old. I had no idea what the name of it was. I had never seen such a weapon.

"What kind of sword is this?" I asked, turning to him. He pulled a small kit out of a top drawer and set it next to his wine glass, then picked up the drink and drained it. A weight I hadn't known had been bearing down on me seemed to ease its way off my shoulders. My heart rate even slowed.

"That, my dear, is an early Eighteenth Century Kaskara from Sudan," he replied somewhat smugly.

"Why isn't it kept in the scabbard? Won't it rust like this?"

"No, in fact, it would rust substantially more if it were kept in its sheath. I found this baby in an antique store when I was in England. The shopkeeper had no idea just what he had and I got it for a steal!"

I have heard the term "geek out" before, but never really thought it allied to normal people, yet here Jack was, totally geeking out on this sword. At some point

I had tuned him out, because he was staring at me as though he just asked a question. I just smiled and nodded; that seemed like the correct response.

He walked over and picked up my left hand. He grabbed my middle finger and began rubbing it. He then opened an alcohol wipe and cleaned my finger. He pricked my finger and it caused me to jump. He collected the ruby drops in a small vile no bigger than a bullet, then set it all aside and looked at me. His gaze bore down on me. There was pure hunger in his eyes and it wasn't for food. *Shit, when will those drugs kick in?*

I took a step back and my back hit the closed door. He followed, putting his hand on the door right next to my head and looking down at me as his other hand slid behind my neck. My head tilted up so I could see him fully.

"Addy, you have been teasing me all night. I am not someone who does well with a tease." The angles of his face seemed to become more pronounced and his eyes bore a hole through my very soul.

"I-I-" I was cut off by the force of his kiss. This was not passion or even lust. There was pure dominance and aggression in his actions. I tried to pull away to run or use my speed, but I couldn't seem to get away. His hand moved down my body. He grabbed and squeezed at my breasts to the point of pain, then dipped his hand lower. He reached the hem of my dress and slowly moved his hand toward my panties. His fingers brushed my sex just before he cupped me fully. Finally, I was able to break his bruising kiss.

"Jack, please, stop," I pleaded, trying to push him away from me. He was immovable. I didn't want to hurt him even though I knew I could. I just wanted this to stop.

He pulled back from me, and with strength and speed I didn't know he had, he threw me on the bed. I had not expected the move, so my reflexes weren't where they should have been. I tried to scramble away, but he was on me before I could get up. He pinned my hands above my head and I felt his firm erection pressing against my pelvis.

"Oh, come on, I know you want it. It will feel good." His words hit me like a freight train. I had heard those exact words from my uncle fifteen years ago. I was suddenly hurled back to that place of hell. I was thrown back to my ten-year-old self.

I was in a new home yet again. But, this time it would be different. Maybe they would be nice. I would do my best not to anger anyone. I would do my best to not get beaten. This was the last place for me to go.

This was my mother's sister. They were actual and real family; they had to love me. Wasn't that like a law or a rule with family?

The first three months were some of the best of my life. But, one night when my uncle visited my room in the middle of the night, he forced my innocence from me. At first it was touching, but it grew to more and I begged for him to stop, but he didn't. The one thing that was my own, he took.

Later, he would tell me things like, "Where will you go?",

"We are family. Who will love you now?", and the worst, "You made me do this. Just look at you. I am only a man."

I snapped back to the present only to realize he was removing my panties. Damn it, I was not ten anymore, but something had been triggered and I couldn't move. It was fear. Pure unadulterated fear, causing every cell in my body to freeze to an impenetrable statue. It was the place I went to when I was a child.

I squeezed my eyes tight. His hands were rough and searching. I couldn't fucking move. Then an image of the way Lachlan looked at me flashed in my mind. He didn't see a helpless child. He saw a strong woman. *I fucking got myself into this, so I need to get myself out of it. I am not ten anymore! I have power.*

I struggled for a small amount of precious space. When that failed, I mentally pictured my hands around his neck. I pulled the invisible ties that I knew were there. His eyes went wide. Then I flexed the mental power even more, until his body floated above me. It gave me just enough room to roll out from underneath him. A few months ago, my telekinetic abilities would have never been strong enough to achieve something like this, at least not with this much control.

I stood up and faced his floating form, flipping him to face up and lowering him to the bed only to see him completely passed out. *Oh shit! Did I kill him?* I ran over to him and searched frantically for a pulse. I felt a strong and steady beating against my two fingers. *Oh thank goodness!*

I plopped down next to him and put my head in my

hands. *This could have been very bad; damn it, Addison.* I stood up, remembering my panties, and retrieved them. I refused to put them back on because he touched them and I didn't want something touching my core that he touched, so I ran my hands along my dress, then remembered there were no pockets. *I have no idea why clothing designers feel like women don't need pockets, but it is damn annoying.* So, I did the next logical thing, stuffed it in my bra. I looked down at Jack, who looked to be sleeping ever so peacefully. I slapped him across the face. Okay, I know it was a low blow to kick someone while they are down and it goes against everything I have been taught and the principles I teach myself. That having been said, fuck him and the horse he rode in on because right now no fucks could be given.

I walked out of the house and didn't look back.

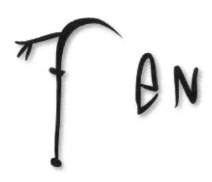

LACHLAN SAT ON THE HOOD OF THE CAR AND looked just as pissed off as when I left him. *Great, just what I need.* I narrowed my eyes at him. His jaw was tight with tension and I could feel how he wanted to explode at me. I was not going to deal with this shit right now. I pulled open the passenger side door and slipped in without a word.

He got behind the wheel and put it in gear. The ride back to my apartment was filled with silence and building anger. The air was charged with the fury I knew just needed a tiny spark to ignite it. I knew what he was doing. He was doing the same thing I was doing: waiting until the door closed behind us. Then all bets were off.

The door of the apartment closed behind me and like a light switch he got in my face and started in on me.

"Just what the fuck were you thinking!?" Our height difference never bothered me until this very moment. He had to bend down to me and looked like he was scolding a mischievous child.

"Addison, you could have been hurt. You could have jeopardized this whole fucking mission; fuck, Addison, you probably already have." He was furious. His eyes went incandescent and the incredulity and strength of his anger slapped me across the face. Even his barely noticeable Scottish burr was more pronounced. But, I did not think he would be breaking out the kilt anytime soon. Damn him. His fists clenched and unclenched.

I looked over to the small coffee table next to the couch that rested against the wall. I calmly walked over to it and climbed atop it, then turned to face him. "I didn't mess fuck-all up. And, had you fucking talked to me at all these last few weeks, maybe I wouldn't have done this. God, Lachlan, what happened to you? What the hell did I do?!" We were the same height now, so he didn't have to bend to get in my face. He walked over and did just that.

"Addison, I have more experience than you. You could have been hurt. What don't you get about that? I know you were panicked at one point. It passed, but I felt your fear pressing on me. What happened?"

"Nothing! He passed out and I was afraid he was dead!" I was so not going into my closet of deepest and darkest secrets with him.

I narrowed my eyes and poked him in the chest with a finger. "Where have you been? You ignore me

145

and reply in a one or two-word text. If you don't like me, fine. Tell Cannon and I'll find another way to work off my favors!" I didn't realize how mad I really was at him until right now. I couldn't even give him the chance to speak, I was that incensed.

"You know what, Lachlan? Fuck you!" I was honest to God yelling at him. My heart was beating like a wild thing. He looked murderous and it only intensified the plains and angles of his face. *Even fighting with him turns me on. What the hell is wrong with me?* His neck was straining, his jaw clenched, his black cotton T-shirt clinging to his muscled chest. The tattoos that covered his arms rippled as he struggled to control himself. I didn't dare look lower for fear of becoming a complete mess.

"You want to know why I haven't been around. You want to know why I have been ignoring you." His eyes traveled down my body as he spoke and his voice took on a harsh guttural tone.

"Yes. Please fucking enlighten me!" My heart rate kicked up a notch and I moved to get off the table. As I jumped off he caught me mid-air with hands under my arms and slammed me against the wall. It didn't hurt, but all my attention was now sure as hell on him. Not that it wasn't before.

"Because I can't fucking keep my hands off of you. And that will be the death of both of us." Then he crushed his lips to mine. I threw my arms around his neck and opened my mouth to him. There were so many fumes in the air and that tiny spark was all it took.

There was nothing soft or gentle about this kiss. It was full of longing and need. *Oh, but the taste of him was intoxicating.* I wrapped my legs around his waist. He growled in response, driving his tongue into my mouth and then retreating quickly. He was staking a claim and taking everything I had and I was letting him. I wasn't just letting him; I needed him to take it, I burned for it.

I opened more to fully accommodate him. Though he was cool to the touch, the heat we generated together was combustible. I ground my hips into him, hoping to feel him. A shot of delicious friction radiated up from my sex and left me throbbing. He slipped his hands from my underarms to my ass and ground himself against me. I could feel him hard against me and became liquid in his arms, completely boneless. I tried to pull his shirt up, but as I did he pulled away from me and sat me down. He pulled his shirt off and as he did, oh God, the muscles that rippled had me about drooling. We were both panting, even though he didn't need it.

"Addison?"

It was a question. Not just a statement. He was asking if I knew there was no going back. I swallowed the lump that had formed in my throat.

"Yes." As soon as the whisper left my lips he was against me in two long steps. He ripped my dress down the back.

"Hey! That was …" He swallowed my next words with a soul-blistering kiss. Dress, what dress? My mind went blank and I couldn't recall any protest I had. This man kissed me to the point of mindlessness.

The dress slipped down my shoulders and fell in tatters to the floor, right along with every bit of good sense I had. He stepped back and looked at me. My cheeks flushed with heat at the expression on his face. His gaze wasn't full of need or lust like one would expect. His eyes were so blue they were almost white; he was hungry. I didn't know if it was for what flowed in my veins or for my body. Either thought along with the expression of such hunger should have made me tuck my tail between my legs and scurry away. But, damn, it only caused my belly to tighten and for me to grow slick with yet more liquid heat. My body was readying for him and I was giving in.

His eyes traveled painfully slowly down my body. His gaze was much like a physical caress, and in its wake left a trail of gooseflesh that caused me to shiver. His eyes widened when he got to the throbbing area between my thighs. He looked up at me and arched an eyebrow. It was at that moment I remembered I had no panties on.

"Don't ask," I murmured in a much huskier voice than I thought was possible. I walked slowly to him and, just before I reached him, I dropped to my knees.

I looked up at him as I reached for the button of his dark-blue jeans. He hissed in a breath as he reached down to run a hand through my hair. Painfully slowly, I popped the button on his jeans loose and then drew the zipper down one agonizing notch at a time. His pants slid down his hips, revealing his large erection, and my throat went dry. He was large, and not just his height.

I wrapped my hand around him and realized that he would burn so good. He had gone completely still in that unnerving way vampires did. I began shaking; I couldn't help it. The way he looked at me with eyes that seemed to pierce my soul.

"Addison, God, I ..." he groaned as I brought the head of his cock to my lips and licked, then slid him fuller into my mouth and suckled him. He felt like silk-covered iron. I ran my tongue up and down his hard length and as I did, I felt him begin to tremble. I held him at the root and squeezed as I sucked him in, tasting his arousal that only fueled my fire. I withdrew him from my mouth to run my tongue along his broad head, growing so wet I would be surprised if it weren't dripping down my thighs. All I would need to do was drop my hand down and press it against my clit and I would come.

He groaned, "Addison, you're going to kill me." I slowly withdrew him from my mouth, sitting back and looking up at him. God, he was an exquisite man. His muscles rippled, crafted from hard work when he was human. His erection jutted out and his testicles were drawn up tight. I leaned back, trying to rip my eyes away from the lower half of him.

He gave me a wicked smile and bent down to kiss me. I opened my mouth to him fully, my heart threatening to beat clear out of my chest. His right hand snaked behind me and, with way more grace than I could have mustered, unclasped my brain one swift motion. *I couldn't even manage that and I have been wearing bras for just about ever! Maybe that is his super power?* It was at that moment when I realized he stilled and was looking down at something in his hand. It was a blue scrap of cloth. My cheeks warmed with flush as it dawned on me what he held. I met his questioning, amused gaze and shrugged.

"Uh, care to explain?" he asked, clearly trying not to laugh.

I narrowed my eyes at him and took the panties, tossed them over my shoulder, and said, "Nope."

I threw my arms around his neck and kissed him. His tongue plunged in and out of my mouth, so much like the sexual act that the ever-present throbbing between my thighs grew stronger and I became wetter still. My hands fingered the hairs at the nape of his neck and tangled in their length. He put a hand at the back of my own neck and eased me to lay back on the floor, breaking our kiss and just sitting there staring at me. While I have never minded being nude, nor have I been self-conscious about my body, the way he looked at me with such fierce intensity almost made me nervous. Like he was a hungry man and I was his meal.

He leaned in and kissed my collarbone, then lowered to my right breast. He paused and I could feel coolness radiating from his lips as they hovered so close without touching. I wanted to arch my back to close the distance. He smiled at me, seeing desperation plastered all over my face.

"Worry not, Addison, I'm going to eat you alive."
He then flicked my nipple with his tongue. A Vampire
just told me he was going to eat me alive and what was
my response? Well, to become mindless with lust and
need. I could no longer resist and arched my back at
him. He took the invitation and sucked the pebbled
flesh into his mouth. Oh, sweet torture, I could feel
his fangs brush against me with every pull and it was
maddening. If I had any good goddamned senses I
would stop this now, but I think I left all good sense on
the floor with the remains of my dress.

His right hand, which had been caressing light
circles along my ribs, made its way to my left breast and
found its pink tip. He pinched at it lightly, then harder,
causing me to cry out in pleasure. His expert fingers
and tongue created a rhythm that had me panting and
begging him for more.

Slowly he drew a line from my breast down my
belly, then settled just above my most private folds.
I arched my hips up in hopes of coaxing him farther
down, but it was to no avail. Finally, after about an
eternity, his hand cupped me. He parted the wet folds
of me until he found my clitoris, then took the stiff
little bud between his fingers and pinched firmly. I
didn't have breath to scream; all I could do was arch
myself up to his touch and groan.

He withdrew my nipple from his mouth and drew
a line with his tongue down my belly. I was throbbing
every place he touched and was being driven to a place
I had never been. I'd been intimate with only a few men

before, but this man was so beyond anything or anyone, I did not know how to react to him.

He had a direct line to my body, hovering just above the fluted folds of my labia as he moaned, "Damn, Addison, you are so gorgeous." Not giving me time to respond, he parted my drenched folds and licked the length of me. And with that long, slow lick of me, my vision blurred. He found my clitoris and pulled it in his mouth and began to suckle at me. Thank goodness for turnabout being fair play, because, sweet mother of God, I was melting into a puddle of my former self.

He began a divesting rhythm of licking, sucking and nipping that had me so close to the edge, I thought I may pass out. His mouth moved higher, causing me to look down at him. He had a wicked smile in his eyes, then without warning he bit me, hard, with his fangs. He had bitten me just above my folds. *Holy fucking hell.* I screamed out as everything throttled me headlong into the most intense orgasm of my life. I had no mind left to think about the fact that he had just bitten me and now drank from me in the most private of areas.

He never stopped; he kept sucking and lapping at me. I couldn't think straight.

"Wait, stop, I, but I ..." I tried to speak, but I didn't know anything anymore. He lifted his head to look up at me. His eyes were nearly white and my blood dripped down his chin. He smiled at me; it was one hundred percent animalistic male satisfaction. He returned to his erotic assault and then I felt his finger slip inside of me. I stopped breathing.

"Oh, Addison, you're so tight," he groaned as he devastated me once again with his tongue and finger. Without warning, he withdrew.

I should have been afraid, but all I could think about was how good he felt and how much I needed him inside of me. He crawled up my body, leaving cool kisses along me that caused a fine tremble to travel in its wake. He hovered above me and I felt his huge erection grind against my aching pelvis. I moaned, not really being able to click my brain into gear, then opened my eyes to see him studying me. He searched my eyes for something. I didn't know what. Then I heard his voice in my mind.

"Addison, there's no going back after this." His voice even mentally was husky with arousal.

I said the only thing my fog-soaked mind could come up with. "Good."

He kissed me with pure abandon. And I kissed him with mindless need. I needed this man at this moment and to be denied would kill me. He shifted my legs farther apart and angled himself at my entrance. His eyes met mine as he lifted my hands above my head and pinned them there with one steely grip. With the other hand he angled my ass and slowly eased into me. He was so damned big and it burned so damned good.

"Oh, Lachlan, I don't think, oh my God …" With every inch he buried deeper in me, my voice and thought retreated.

Once he was fully inside me, he ground his pelvis against me, somehow putting pressure on my aching little bud. He withdrew, leaving me panting for more. Then without preamble, he drove into me. He began this rhythm of filling me, grinding, then withdrawing, leaving me breathless and crazed. The pressure that was building reached a near-fever pitch.

He moved his hand from my ass to find my clit, rubbing me as he drove into me over and over. The pain from his bite and the pleasure of having him inside me made for a maddening mix. I tilted my head to the side and offered the last thing I had to him. There was no thought, as my mind had left the building long ago, and he didn't hesitate.

Lachlan bit me and I flew apart. The French call this *la petite mort,* or the little death. The moment of orgasm, of one so strong that surely death would follow, and now I knew why. It was a feeling beyond myself, a feeling I wasn't sure I could come back from. He groaned against my neck then threw his head back and called my name. I pulsed around him as he pulsed inside of me, giving me every last drop that he had to offer. He dropped his forehead to mine and we both lay there trying to pick up the pieces of ourselves.

He had destroyed me. Every wall I had erected lay in rubble at my feet. I didn't even know what to call what we had just done. Sex seemed too simple. Love making? No way. Fucking? Didn't even come close. This man created a whole new category.

He still lay buried in me when he lifted his head and said huskily, "Fucking hell, Addison."

"Yeah, that," was all I could manage. He released

my hands and I ran them down his face.

"He will kill me and possibly kill you for this," he asserted as he searched my eyes, looking for regret about what we had done, or possibly fear. Well, he wouldn't find it. He moved off and out of me in one motion. Strangely, it left me feeling empty.

I had no idea what to do now. He had just demolished me to the point where I didn't think walking was on the agenda. I rolled on my side to face him.

"I don't … umph." He pulled me on top of him so we lay torso to torso and smiled at me, then pulled my head to rest on his shoulder. He began running his fingers through my hair. It was a strangely tender moment that certainly did not create thousands of little butterflies in my stomach. It didn't.

"You were saying?" His voice rumbled in his chest against my ear.

"I don't think he will kill us," I said drawing a circle around his flat, tanned nipple.

Lachlan went very still. Not that he wasn't always unmoving, because he didn't need to breathe, but this was unnerving. I shifted to look at his face. His expression was grave. Then mentally he remarked, "You need to understand something. Cannon wants you, he was very clear with me. And it has never been an issue, but, Addison, you don't know him like you think you do."

"Why does he want me so badly? I'm not that special," I asked, trying to keep my mental voice steady and even.

He gently rolled me off of him, stood up, and walked into the bedroom. I heard him pull the bed down, so I got up and walked in only to smack right into him. The impact caused me to go sprawling to the floor. My ass hit the ground and my legs went wide. I was a bit dazed.

"Shit, I'm sorry. I am faster than I'm used to, thanks to your blood," he said, bending over me. He helped me up and, in doing so, he pulled me into his arms. I was not going to think about how good it felt to be there. I wasn't. *Shit!*

"It's okay. It takes getting used to," I replied, looking up at his face. I couldn't meet his eyes, afraid of falling into their depths. And if I fell I knew just as sure as I needed air in my lungs that I would never be able to pull myself out again. So, instead I started at his lips. His full, kissable lips that had just been on my ... *Shit, this is not helping.*

"A lot of it had to do with you having been bound to him. We are very territorial creatures. But, Addison …" He angled my face to his. His expression went from concerned to hard in an instant. "... He mainly wants you for the same reasons I do. And now I don't know how to give you back to him." He kissed me, lightly at first, but then it deepened into something more. A gentle throb began to pulse between my legs. Gracious, this man did things to my inhibitions that no one could do. I pulled away and looked at him.

"I don't want you to get hurt. But, when this is over…" I trailed off, not able to finish the damn statement. I tried to swallow the damned lump that had settled there, but it didn't work.

"We will figure it out. Because the thought of cutting our ties is one thing, but giving you to him? Fuck that," he snarled.

I tried to hide a smile. "Okay, what time is it?"

"Late. Come, let me take you to bed," he said, leading me to the bedroom. I bent down to snag the panties laying on the floor.

Lachlan grabbed them from me and smiled.

"You won't be needing these." He got into the bed and tossed them over his shoulder. I smiled and climbed in with him.

"Oh, wait!" I paused. "I'm not on, um, birth control. Can you?" I mean, I have never heard of it. But, I don't know everything.

He shook his head and replied, "No, Addison. I can't get you with child. It has only happened twice before and both were Vampires. I don't know the logistics of it, so don't ask."

I snuggled closer to him and he held me tighter. I shivered at the intimacy of the scene, slowly drifting off to sleep.

Eleven

LARGE HANDS ROAMED MY BODY. THEY WERE COOL to the touch, causing me to shake as they pinched and rubbed me to a frenzy. I never saw a face, but I knew whose hands they were.

Cannon stroked me in the most intimate of places, both on my body and in my mind. I could feel myself growing wet and it was driving me to a fever pitch. His touch wasn't just physical, but mental. It should have scared me that he could reach me in this way, but I was too sleep fogged for it to register.

He pulled me deeper into the dream, and every time I managed to convince myself to wake up, he sent an electric shock of pleasure through my body and mind to erase all thought. His dark silhouette hovered over me. Then he descended upon me. I woke up gasping for air.

What the royal hell was that? I looked over to the

bedside table. The clock read 4:53 PM. Lachlan lay nearly on top of me. I scooted out from our tangled limbs as carefully as I could. Shit, I was so going to be fired. I had forgotten to call in, again. I found Lachlan's black shirt crumpled on the floor, picked it up, and slipped it over my head. It hung to my knees, but hey, it would work for now.

I walked into the kitchen to find my phone. Four missed calls. Two from the dojo, two from Kyle. Ugh, I did not want to deal with Kyle. I dialed the number to the dojo.

"Addison, you better have an amazing excuse." Darryl's rich baritone voice sounded over the speaker. *He is pissed.* He was like a father and it hurt my heart to upset him.

"Darryl, I am so sorry. I should have called. I have been," I looked over at the bedroom door, "detained."

"Addison, I have respected your privacy and never asked you questions about your past. That having been said, I know you're involved with Cannon Blackwood and I'm going to just come out and say it…" He paused and I tried to brace myself for whatever it was that he was going to hit me with. "Do I need to drug test you?"

There was no bracing for that question. It hit me with the impact of a physical blow. It even knocked the wind out of me. I gripped the counter to keep myself upright. I was in shock, shifting from anger at Darryl to myself and then settling on Cannon.

It was impossible to keep the emotion I was feeling out of my voice so I didn't even try. "If that is something you would like to do, I can go to a testing center now." It wasn't about keeping my job. I mean, that was part of it, but it was about proving to him that I was clean and had been for over seven years.

"Goddamn it, Addison! I don't know what you're involved in, but I know it's bad. I know you won't tell me, but for God's sake, let me know you're safe." His voice was full of emotion.

Tears pricked my eyes. "I love you, Darryl, and I am safe. This is something I have no choice about. I know you can't hold my job but…"

"Oh, shut up. Just call me and check in. I mean it, Addison, or I'll come looking for you. Oh and Kyle may be stopping by. I told him I hadn't heard from you and he said he would check on you for me."

"Okay, I'll call you to check in. And I'll call Kyle and tell him I'm fine. I have been meaning to talk to him anyway."

"Yeah, because that boy has it bad for you. Be nice when you break his heart."

"Yeah, I know." There was a soft tentative knock at the door. My stomach dropped to my feet, knowing who was on the other side of that door. I sighed and told Darryl goodbye.

I took a deep breath to ready myself for what was about to happen.

KYLE STOOD AT MY DOOR HOLDING A BOUQUET OF red roses. A few things flashed in my mind as I saw him standing there. *Oh the poor shmuck. I am a horrible human being. Don't be a chicken shit, Addison.* I gave him a sweet smile.

"Kyle, what are you doing here? How did you get in?" I asked, stepping into the hallway. I mostly shut the door behind me.

"Hey, your neighbor let me in. And Darryl asked me to come by. He's worried about you," he stated, leaning in for a kiss. I turned my head slightly and he kissed my cheek.

"Yeah, I just spoke with him. Sorry to make y'all worry. I am just dealing with personal issues," I said, crossing my arms around my middle.

"Look ..."

"Here ..." We both started at the same time.

"Thank you, they are lovely," I replied as he handed me the flowers.

"Addison, I know you have something going on, but I need to tell you how I feel about you." He glanced down at my exposed feet. It was at that moment I remembered I was standing in my hallway with no pants on, or panties for that matter. My face grew warm with flush.

"Wait, Kyle, listen. I don't ... uft." Strong arms snaked around my waist and pulled me through my apartment door. The sudden jolt caused me to drop the flowers. Just as the door slammed shut I whirled to find Lachlan seething and snarling at the door.

"What the hell are you doing?" I demanded, smacking a hand on his bare chest.

161

"That little twerp has a hard-on for you." He spat the words, clearly displeased at Kyle's presence. *Yeah, well, me too, bub.*

"You cannot just slam doors in people's faces!" I glanced down and realized he was butt naked. My eyes widened at the sight and my heart picked up its pace.

"Yes, I can."

"Oh lord, listen, please go put pants on. I can't think with you standing here nude," I barked, diverting my eyes. I just needed to think about something not sexy. Like trees, or public bathrooms.

He took a step forward and I threw a hand up as if to hold him off. I narrowed my eyes at him and lowered my voice. "I will deal with him, but you cannot act like a Neanderthal! Or so help me God, Lachlan, I will do what I did to you the first time we met."

He bent down and kissed my nose before he turned and walked into the bedroom. I whirled and threw the door open. *Why? Why can't this just be easy? Ugh!* I opened to find Kyle standing there looking severely ticked.

"You know what, Addison, I think I'll let you start," he said, not meeting my eyes. I didn't want to hurt him. But, my not wanting to hurt him had only prolonged this.

"Kyle, I am so sorry. I just, it's just …" I couldn't make myself say it.

"Let me guess, it's not you, it's me?" His words stung with venom.

"I just don't feel anything for you other than

friendship." There, I said it. Shouldn't it have made me feel better?

"Yeah, that's kind of obvious now, isn't it?" he asked, pointing to the door.

"I'm sorry, Kyle, I should have told you sooner." I was the one who couldn't meet his eyes now.

"Yeah, you sure as hell should have." He turned and walked down the stairs. I leaned against my door and softly banged my head against the wood.

Karma. That had to be it. This had to be karma smacking me down. I didn't want to be a mean person or hurt people, but at every turn lately it just seemed like I made one mistake after another. For seven years my life had made its way back to the train tracks and now I felt like I was derailing and there was nothing I could do but stand back and watch the train wreck happen.

I walked back into my apartment and clearly there was a small silver lining to this cloud, as the scent of coffee assaulted and tickled my nose. I could have died happy at the sight of the steaming mug on the coffee table. I picked it up and took a sip. The rich liquid scalded my lips and tongue, but oh sweet mother of all that was holy, it was so worth it. I moaned into the cup, it was that good.

I felt Lachlan behind me. His hand wrapped around my waist as he pressed his pelvis snug against me, his erection firm against my ass. I was still sore from last night. He was inexhaustible.

"Do you need to eat?" My voice was husky despite

everything.

He nipped at my ear then kissed my neck, causing me to suck in a breath. "Oh yes, I do."

"I-I-I oh God ..." I moaned. My eyes fluttered shut. Just as they closed, they flew open with a thought

"Jack!" I felt him pause. "Jack, I never told you what I found out about him!"

Lachlan grudgingly let me go so I could get a little distance from him. I could seriously not form a coherent thought with him that close to me.

I sat down on the couch and told him everything that had happened, though I left out the sexual advances. I tried reading his face but he went into that stony Vampire expression. *I wish I could do that. Just shut off all emotional expressions. I bet I should never play poker with him.*

"They either have a Vampire locked up they are forcing to change people, something I find highly unlikely, or they have a drug that they are using to turn people. He was completely smashed; there is no way he remembers telling me anything."

"That has to be it," Lachlan snarled the words. He began to pace the length of my small apartment.

"Lachlan, why is it so bad that pushers are changed?" The question had been nagging me for some time.

"It's a balance of power. We develop powers the older we get. Think of it like giving a toddler the ability to drive but still in the mind of a toddler."

"I'm not sure I understand."

"We develop our powers over time. This gives

us time to cope with our new abilities and hunger. Pushers already have so much power that they could be a danger. They have the hunger and no way to control it. And they are incredibly powerful."

"It's not like a toddler with the ability to drive, but the ability to kill and no way to stop them." *Holy shit.*

"Exactly, we need to call the team and set things in motion. We need to get this drug out of their hands and destroy all record of it."

Without thinking about it, I got up and walked over to him. He, too, seemed to be caught off-guard. But, damn it, I liked him. I stood in front of him so closely that I could feel coolness radiating off of him. I walked my finger across the horizontal line of his pants and looked up into his penetrating gaze.

"Are you hungry?" My voice was rough with arousal. I tilted my head to the side and brushed my sleep-tangled hair to the side. I felt exposed to this Vampire, but I trusted him. Even though I knew I shouldn't.

I heard a growl low in his chest. I stepped closer, closing the last few inches that separated us. He was hard and cool. It was a strange combination. But, one that I was fast coming to crave. It thrilled me to push him like this.

His hands started at my ass and ran up my body slowly until they cradled my face. His eyes sparked with what was fast becoming a look that drove me wild. Anticipation.

"Addison, I can't get enough of you." He tilted my head, further exposing yet more of me to him. I knew he could see my pulse fluttering. He placed a small, cool kiss to the jumping beat. Then, so lightly, he brushed his lips across my skin and I trembled. I couldn't help it and he knew it. He eased his fangs into my neck so achingly slowly. I felt a small moan escape my lips.

With every pull, pain bloomed and died in the very same moment, replaced with sensual heat. Then, suddenly, he groaned and collapsed to the floor, clutching at his abdomen. My hand flew to my neck to help slow the trickles of blood. *Shit, what happened?* Holding my neck, I bent down and put a hand on him.

"Lachlan, what's wrong?" He met my eyes and the expression in his gaze sent chills wracking through me.

"Cannon." It was the only word I could make out between groans and grunts.

Finally, as though nothing was wrong, Lachlan stood up. *What the flying hell just happened?* He walked into the bedroom and came out carrying some of my workout clothes. Okay, now was not the time to spar or do jumping jacks.

Before I could speak he stated coolly, with complete detachment, "Cannon pulled me. He wants an update. Get dressed."

Here he was going from hot to cold and it pissed me off. For shit's sake, I don't just sleep with someone for the hell of it. Well, if he thought I would let him get away with that bullshit he had another thing coming. I was going to make this as difficult for him as possible. I narrowed my eyes at him and pulled his shirt over my head, then walked over and pressed the shirt against his chest.

"Here, this is yours." I stood there completely nude in front of him. His gaze went electric. I turned to go get dressed, but his hand grabbed my arm and yanked me back.

"What are you doing?" His voice was severe.

"Going to get dressed." I spat the words. I tried to be civil about this, but how could I be? I did not sign up to ride roller coaster Lachlan. I tried to pull my arm from his but it was impossible, so instead I sighed and met his gaze.

"Don't shut me out. I don't know what we are doing, but I'm in it as long as you are." The words seemed to flow out before I could stop them.

"I just don't want to see you hurt. And this will get you hurt," he replied with unequivocal resolution.

"Would you rather see me with Cannon?" I knew it was petty, but I still couldn't stop myself from saying it.

"No!" It was a snarl.

I put my hand over the one gripping my arm. "Good, then stop the hot and cold. You're either in this with me or not." I honestly didn't know how I felt. I mean, I wasn't ready to pick out China patterns or bridesmaid dresses. But I knew this back and forth had to stop.

He searched my eyes for a moment before he sighed and dropped his hand from my arm.

"I'm in this. Whatever this is. Please go get dressed. He wants you there too."

Ugh, great. My mind went back to the dream I had.

As I was dressing I asked, "Hey, I had a weird dream about Cannon last night." I tried to say it as though it didn't bother me, though the reality was different. I pulled some cotton shorts over my hips and grabbed the sneakers by the door. Heading over to the couch, I sat down to slip them on when I saw Lachlan staring at me.

"What kind of dream?" I didn't know what it was in his voice but it set off little alarm bells.

"Uh, well," I said, not meeting his eyes, "it was a sex dream. I couldn't see his face, but I knew it was him. I didn't mean to dream about it. But, every time I tried to wake up I seemed to be pulled deeper."

"Shit. Cannon. Damn it."

"What?" I asked tying my shoelaces.

"It's part of his mind-reading abilities. He can also enter into humans' dreams."

My mouth fell open. I closed it with a clack of teeth, incensed. I couldn't believe it. Incredulity was too small a word for my utter and complete shock.

"I think I need to talk with Cannon," I snarled through clenched teeth.

CIVILITY WAS NOT AN ATTRIBUTE I WAS CURRENTLY capable of. Yet, here we were. Cannon, Lachlan, and myself standing in his den. Living room? I had no idea what to call this room. The whole way here, I plotted and planned out just what I would say to this damn Vampire. I tried, I really did, but my give a damn was so fucking busted that there was no going back.

"What the fuck do you want, Cannon?" I guess I didn't try hard enough because the words sliced the air.

His smile was one of knowing. I had to stifle a shudder under his gaze. Then it fell away, giving me a glance at the monster that lay beneath the suit and tie. I took a step back.

"Oh, Addison, I'm hurt." He covered his shriveled heart with his hand and mock hunched over as though he were in pain. "I had hoped after what we shared last night you would be very happy to see me."

"You had no right." It was a bare whisper. *Great way to stand firm, Addison.* This was not at all going how I planned.

"She's so cute, isn't she?" he asked, completely ignoring me.

"Brother, what do you want?" Lachlan replied, clearly annoyed.

"You have one week to finish this." Cannon walked behind the bar and poured some vermouth into a metal mixing cup.

"Cannon, it's not that easy."

"Well, stop fucking around." He glared at me in such a way that left me feeling exposed. Returning to his concoction, he asked, "What do you know?"

Lachlan filled him in on the things we knew and the guesses we made. He told him his plan.

"We know the head geneticist has a thing for Addison, so that gives us an in. I need to confirm with my team, but one week should be sufficient time to complete this."

Cannon went still while Lachlan explained the details of the information we had.

"Have they been successful in changing any pushers? The reports on TV are getting worse. The crime rate is higher than it has ever been."

"We don't know. But based on that information, I think it's safe to assume, yes," I said before Lachlan had time.

"The amount of weaponry they have been buying has tripled in the last week. If this is all correct, it might be safe to assume that they are creating an army." An army? What for?

"Jack may be developing this drug, but he's not the puppet master. Someone big has to be pulling his strings," I guessed.

"Let's not jump to conclusions just yet. Brother, let us finish this. There will be a money trail and we will see where that leads." Lachlan walked over to the bar and took one of the three martinis Cannon poured. He downed it in one swallow.

"We done?" he asked, setting the glass down.

"Almost, one other thing."

Much like the strike of a cobra, Cannon punched his brother square in the jaw. Without thought I ran to Lachlan, who was slumped on the floor, but just before I got to him he lifted his arm in a stop motion. I halted where I stood, a foot away from him, and glared at Cannon. What the hell was his problem?

"What is wrong with you, Cannon?" I was livid.

Yeah, we all know he is powerful as shit, but there is no need to just be an ass because you can.

Cannon walked around the bar, all the while assessing me. Apparently he did not like what he saw, because with every step he took, his gaze became more intense and his jaw tightened in a hard white line. It actually caused me to take a step back. *Stupid! You don't run from a predator, that's a great way to get eaten.* And I really did not want to be eaten.

I found what little starch I could muster and injected it into my spine, crossing my arms over my chest and sticking out a hip. Okay, I know it was more of a teenager with an attitude stance, but it was as good as I was going to get. *Hey, fake it 'til you make it, right?*

He didn't stop. He walked right up to me and ducked his head to my throat and breathed in. My heart started a wild and erratic beat. Then he did something that caught me so off-guard I almost passed out. He began laughing. A deep, rich sound that filled the room. It sent a shiver through me. What the hell was so funny? He stumbled back away from me as though he could barely stand up straight due to his immense laughter. I looked over to Lachlan, who was pulling himself off the floor. He looked just as confused as I felt.

"Oh, that is rich!" Cannon bellowed between guffaws. "Lachlan! Look at her!"

I was taken aback. Look at me? What the hell did I do? Lachlan looked over at me and shrugged. He held a hand over his jaw where Cannon hit him.

"Oh, oh, you don't see it! Oh, Lachlan. This is going

to be good. Look. At. Her. Lachlan."

"Cannon, I don't know what you're getting at. How about you clue us in," Lachlan, asked with a confused look still on his face.

"You fucked her, didn't you?" We both went quiet. Cannon lost it again. This was not the reaction I thought we would get when Cannon found out.

"You didn't tell her, did you? And look at her looking all protective of you. She may even love you. And you didn't even tell her." He looked from Lachlan to me and back again. I glanced at Lachlan. His face went pale.

Despite what Cannon said, I did not love Lachlan. Well, I didn't think I did. We so weren't to that point. But, what hadn't Lachlan told me?

"Addison, listen, I need to tell you something. I should have told you before we got involved." Lachlan's voice was rushed in my mind. I tried to shut down the connection to him. All of the blood seemed to drain from my body. I felt cold and exposed.

"What didn't he tell me, Cannon?" My voice was calm and measured, completely contrary to how I was seething and boiling on the inside.

"Oh, yes, I think I want to be the one to tell her." Cannon was clearly pleased with himself.

Lachlan took a few steps toward me and in my head he was yelling my name, but I ignored him and set all of my attention to Cannon and his next words.

"He can't ever love you. He is consort to Merriam Little, Mistress of Chicago." It was a punch in the gut that knocked the breath out of me.

The word *consort* ricocheted off the sides of my skull like some kind of horrific pinball. I had no idea what the term meant. But, one thing was clear. I had been misled. I prided myself on the fact that I was a good judge of character and that I did not give myself to just anyone. I didn't love him. But, I thought, I could have.

I closed my eyes and took a deep breath in and held it. Maybe if I just didn't breathe. Maybe if I could hold on to this breath long enough the next one, the one with all of the disappointment, would simply never come. I straightened my spine, let out the breath and opened my eyes.

"What is a consort?" My tone was utterly passionless and disconnected.

Cannon raised his eyebrow at me and stated, "Lachlan is bound to me because I am his maker, but he is bound to Merriam because he is her lover."

"Cannon! I have not been her lover in nearly one hundred and fifty years. Addison, there is more to it than that. He is just trying to use this as a tactic so he can keep you."

Cannon's laughter filled the room yet again. The sound seemed to fill my mouth and nose, causing me to choke. I didn't want to hear any of this.

"Lachlan, I told you when you came here asking to bind her to you. And Addison, you have known this for seven years. She is mine. And nothing you do or say will change that." His tone went completely cold and measured.

My ears were ringing. There was this annoying buzzing that I realized was Lachlan's mental voice screaming at me. I ignored it and looked at Cannon. He was the picture of smugness. Completely satisfied with himself.

"Are we done here?" I wanted to get out of this place so badly my legs were shaking.

"Yes, you have one week."

I walked toward the door when I felt a hand on my shoulder. I shuddered, knowing it was Lachlan. Stepping to the side, I brushed his hand off my shoulder.

I didn't have to say a word, mentally or otherwise; he knew what I was feeling. He walked past me toward the door. Just as I was about to leave, Cannon's iron grip tightened around my upper arm. I turned and gave him an annoyed look.

"What, Cannon?" I was so sick of dealing with these Vampires; I just wanted to be done. My chest hurt. My head was throbbing and my heart was laying in a bloody mess on the floor. His hand tightened to the point of pain, but I refused to flinch.

"Why do you care so much, Cannon? You have not contacted me in nearly six years, yet here you are snarling that I am yours." This bugged me so much, I had to ask him. I gritted my teeth as his grip on me tightened.

"How naive are you? Do you really think that I haven't been watching you this whole time? Who owns the building where your dojo is located? Who are you really paying rent to? I am never, nor have I ever been far away from you." At his words my stomach dropped. He had been watching me this whole time? Shit, had my life ever really been my own? The money for the renovations on the dojo had to have come from him. It infuriated me.

He leaned close to me. I felt his cool lips against my ear and the puff of his breath as he spoke the words that chilled my bones, "Fuck him all you want." He kissed my neck. It was feather light yet caused a shiver to wrack my body. He pulled me closer to him and sucked my earlobe into his mouth. Despite everything, my knees trembled and, damn it, I was not getting turned on. I just wasn't. He released his hold on my ear.

"But, remember in the end, Addison. You. Are. Mine." His words clung to my skin.

I tried to yank my arm from his, but he held on. Finally, he let go, making it blazingly clear that he was letting me go on his terms and his terms alone. Also, in that moment, I had an uninterrupted view of my future. And I was so very screwed.

Twelve

Whatever the tactic, I couldn't stand looking at Lachlan. He hadn't lied to me, not in the traditional sense anyway. But wasn't there such a thing as lying by omission? I was hurt. I felt mislead. It honestly surprised me just how hurt I was. Maybe it was a good thing. Hell, I was falling for this guy way too fast. I needed time to sort through all of this crap I found myself in anyway. Maybe I only felt something for him because he was the first person I had slept with in seven years. That was it. It had to be.

Resolution settled in my bones, yet my heart still ached with a dull throb. The last thing I wanted to do was see him or hear anything he had to say. But I would not be some hurt twit. I would not be a brat. I could be big about this.

"Addison," Lachlan's voice broke through my mental barrier, jolting me out of my thoughts.

I looked at him and gave him my best passionless gaze and coupled it with my *eat shit and die* tone. "What?"

"Please, let me explain everything, and if you decide you hate me and never want to see me again after this job, I won't push you." There was something in his tone I couldn't place, supplication maybe?

"I really have nothing to say to you, nor do I care what you have to say." I pushed past him and walked into my kitchen. I looked at the microwave. It was 7:26 PM. The exchange at Cannon's only took thirty or so minutes.

I needed coffee. I needed it set up in an IV bag and inserted directly into my veins. Barring that, a cup would have to do. I picked up the half-full pot and poured it into a mug. The liquid had cooled substantially, but I couldn't complain. Everyone would be here in about thirty minutes. I had no idea when my apartment became meet-up central, but it was getting old. This job could not be done soon enough.

"Addison! Please." I looked up to find him standing far too close. His blue eyes sparkled. I looked away, not wanting to think he was beautiful. I sipped my coffee and pushed past him, yet again, and went to sit on the couch. I pulled my legs up under me and waved my hand at him to continue.

"Damn it, Addison, if I thought it mattered at all, don't you think I would have told you?"

I sealed my emotions off. I would not give him one more glimpse at how he made me feel or how much pain I was really in. He sighed and continued. "I have no idea where to start. So, I guess I'll start from the beginning."

"I was changed by Cannon in 1644. I knew what he was. Our mother never talked about him, but the people in the town where I lived did. I was born only a few years after he was reborn as a Vampire. Cannon's father left before he was born and mine stayed. My mother told me he left before she and my father met, but that when Cannon found out she remarried, he was distraught, though I have no idea why. I did not know my brother back then, nor do I know how he was changed. He won't tell anyone. All I knew of my brother was that he was a monster who wasn't welcome in our home. In fact, I did not meet him until the day he changed me. Anyway, fast forward to 1644. In Scotland, that was a particularly brutal time. I was twenty-eight and preparing to go to war. Between 1644 and 1651 were the wars of the three kingdoms. But it was 1644 to about 1645, when Scotland was involved in a civil war, that my life changed. During the civil war, you had the royalists who supported Charles I and a man named James Graham. Then you had the Covenanters, who supported the English parliament. There may have been civil war and unrest, but frankly, most people just wanted to be with their clans and live the life they had been living. I never made it to fight in any battle or war."

His face was shadowed with remembered pain. I wanted to reach out and touch him, but I didn't. It was such a feeling of duality to want to comfort him and be livid with him at the same time.

"I was leaving town. This was about three hundred and seventy years ago, so my memories are a little fuzzy. I don't recall why I was leaving. Maybe to meet up with a girl. That sounds a lot like me." He quickly added, "Or at least how I was."

I gnashed my teeth at the admission, but refused to let it show on my face.

"I had not a single care in the world. I was going to go fight in the war soon and had many beautiful lovers. I was to meet someone, I think, under a large Birnam oak tree just outside town. I could have been just taking a walk. Like I said, I don't recall, but when I got there it, was Cannon waiting for me. It was like he knew I would be there. He told me who he was and offered to change me. I think he was trying to get me to trust him. I told him no. I did not want to be a monster like him. I did not want to be hated by my mother and father. He attacked me and I woke up like this. Cannon enjoys the monster inside him." He didn't meet my eyes when he added, "But, I hate what I am."

"Jesus." The word slipped out before I could stop it. I didn't want to care about him or how he was changed. Cannon really was a brutal bastard.

He smiled at me and continued. "My family was ripped from me, as was the only life I had known. For years, I traveled with Cannon and for years, I hated him. But I had nowhere else to go. About one hundred years after my turn, we found ourselves in Paris. That's where we crossed paths with a nasty master Vampire named La petite Merriam. I thought I was in love with her. But the reality was far simpler. She was much more powerful than Cannon and I knew she could kill him. I allied myself with her and left Cannon's side. I became her consort a long time ago."

"Wait, how is Cannon Master if she is more powerful?" I really didn't understand how this Vampire structure worked.

"She has been in a ..." he struggled for a word, "... trance ... for some time. Cannon isn't the most powerful or the oldest. He is powerful, don't get me wrong. But, he was the one who wanted the job and no one stronger or older wanted the job."

"Oh, okay." Damn. I was angry at him, needed to protect myself, but here I was being all interested in what he was saying.

"My time with Merriam was spent doing things I wish I hadn't."

"Like what?" I needed to know. I'm not sure I *wanted* to know, but I needed it.

"Addison, I don't want you to think any less of me for what I did in my past." His voice was laced with shame.

"Lachlan, tell me." I would not budge on this point. He must have seen it in my eyes, because he let out a breath of resignation. Any breath he took in or let out was always unnerving, because it reminded me that he really was not like me.

"When I feed, it's a strange mix of emotions and

tastes. First it's sour, then sweet. The closer the human gets to death, the sweeter it gets. Addison, we killed a lot of people. We played with them." He closed his eyes and continued, "We traveled the world and in our wake was a river of blood and bodies."

I flinched. I couldn't help it. I knew what he was. I knew he had killed, all of the old ones had. But the thought of Lachlan, who had the ability to heal, killing so many jarred me.

"Is that what you wanted to hear? Does that help you hate me more?" He was hurt, but damn it, so was I. I looked away from him. Maybe that's why I needed to know. I was so confused about all of this.

"Lachlan, why didn't you tell me?" I wasn't his girlfriend or lover or whatever, but I deserved to know!

"Being her consort was great, for the first years anyway. I think the best part was knowing how it chafed Cannon. But, I came to realize I did not want to be her consort, so I asked for her to break the ties. She not only refused, but made the next years a living hell. She has been in her trance for over one hundred years. It hasn't been an issue until now. Cannon would much rather take you by drawing you to him rather than be seen as the bad guy and take you by force." His lips pursed into a white line; clearly he wanted to say more, but stopped.

"Cannon said you couldn't love me. What did he mean?" This was the question I needed answered. Cannon could have just said he's with someone else and didn't tell you. But the way he phrased it was so strange.

Lachlan shifted, clearly uncomfortable with the question. *Well, you know what, buddy, this whole fucked-up situation is uncomfortable, so suck it up, buttercup.*

"Addison …" He had that petulant tone and it pissed me off.

"Lachlan, cut the crap."

"I am not human and I haven't been in a long time. I don't feel human emotions like you do. Love isn't something I can offer anyone. I can't love."

I can't love. I had seen emotion cross his face more than once. *I can't love.* The words echoed through the room; they carried such weight with them, they filled the space, making me feel small and insubstantial. He couldn't or wouldn't? I didn't want to label what we shared, but I also didn't want the possibility of love or whatever this could have been taken from me. My eyes burned and my chest felt tight. Every breath I was able to effectively take felt like an achievement.

I stood up and crossed the room. I walked to the door and opened it, needing to get out of this room. It was stagnate with those words. But regardless, crying wouldn't happen. I would never be that weak again, no matter the situation.

I paused at the door and called over my shoulder, "I need air. I'll be back. Start without me. Oh, and Gen is welcome in my home."

I turned and walked away, slamming up what little mental defenses I had. I wanted nothing to do with life right now and for me there was one escape. I ran. I ran as fast and far as I could.

I HAD NO IDEA WHERE I WOULD END UP, BUT WHEN I got there, the place shocked me like a slap in the face. I stood in front of a rat's nest of an apartment complex in downtown Atlanta. This was the place I would come to shoot up. I would buy and use in this disgusting place. Why had I come here? I avoided this place like the plague.

There are twelve steps in NA, much like AA. I had been through all of them and held fast to them over these seven years. I have never fallen off the wagon, so to speak. But the temptation was always there. It was a voice in the back of my head telling me that one more time wouldn't hurt, because now I knew I could stop. One time wouldn't hurt anything. Just one little time.

Now, standing here, my mouth watered. I kept myself rooted to the ground; I feared that if I moved even an inch, I would go in. My skin felt like it was on fire and I began to ache deep in my bones. Ugh, I hadn't wanted drugs like this in a long time. Hell, I rarely took Tylenol or Ibuprofen. *There's something about the needle, how it feels sliding into your skin. Knowing that in moments your whole world is about to spin out of control, but your body, oh your body.* I shuddered at the mere thought of it.

I shook my head, trying to rid it of the remembered ecstasy of what it felt like to get high. When that didn't work, I brought up that image of me tied up on a dirty mattress. Then I remembered the feeling I had when

Darryl asked if he needed to drug test me. That did it.

I ran again. I needed to run to a place where nothing could follow me. I had nowhere to go.

"Addison." Lachlan's mental voice caused me to pause.

"Get out of my head." I tried to put my mental defenses up, but he broke through them.

"Please, I can feel how conflicted and confused you are. You're in pain and it's killing me."

He can feel me? Shit! "Leave me alone. I'll be there soon."

"Goddamn it, Addison. I may not be able to love, but you make me feel things. You left before I could tell you. You make me feel and remember what being human is like. Please stop shutting me out. The team is here now, we have a job to do, and once it's done I have to give you back to Cannon and you will never have to see me again." His voice was firm and resolute.

"I am not some jacket to be returned when you're done with me!"

"Damn it! Addison, I know this, but that is how Cannon sees you and he will not stop until you're in his bed." He sounded frustrated. *Yeah well, me too.*

"I don't know what I want, Lachlan." It was the truth. My mind was swimming in a sea of questions, comments and confusion. I felt like I was drowning.

"I understand, but please, let's not look too far ahead of what this is. Let's just finish this job and see where we are. Please come back."

I sighed and ran back to my home. Home was

where the Vampire was, right? *Maybe I should get a framed cross stitch to that effect.*

GEN STOOD OUTSIDE OF MY DOOR, LEANING ON ITS frame.

"Finally, would you please invite me in, for fuck's sake? You have kept me waiting for twenty damn minutes," Gen seethed. She always seethed. If you looked up the word in the dictionary you would see her face, seething. She wore a cat suit of white tight leather. Where on Earth does one find a white leather cat suit? Furthermore how did she squeeze herself in it? It was honestly perplexing.

"Oh, Gen, you're here, goodie goodie gumdrops. Please won't you come in?" I asked in my best fake tone I could manage.

She looked me over and her eyes widened at the sight of my hair. She opened her mouth for what I am sure was a pithy comment about how insane my hair was, but I held up a hand and walked in.

I was greeted by Theo's smiling face. Unable to help myself, I smiled back and threw my arms around him for a hug.

I looked up to him and whispered softly, "I am so sorry for getting you in trouble."

"Nah, don't worry about it." He squeezed me tighter.

Lachlan coughed, clearing his throat. "Okay, let's make a plan." He eyed Theo's arm that was still resting on my shoulder with obvious disdain. I tried to hide my smile but failed, enjoying the fact that he was jealous. *You're mad, Addison, remember?*

Lachlan glared at me and began telling the rest of the team what I learned when I was with Jack. When he was done the team had looks of incredulity, horror and appreciation plastered across their faces.

"Wow," Brent finally managed.

"This job just got a lot more complicated," Theo added, running a large hand over his bald head.

"Fucking humans. They think they know everything about what we are. They have been so fucking sheltered. If they knew the truth, they would be peeing in their pants," Gen shouted, clearly pissed off with the situation. I opened my mouth to inform her that there were humans in the room, but Theo caught my eye and shook his head at me, telling me to shut up. I shut my mouth, thinking that maybe this would only add fuel to the fire.

"Gen, you have been looking into the specs on the buildings. What can you tell us?" Lachlan asked, walking over to my small coffee table. On it were tubes and unrolled blueprints of the compound spread across the small surface.

"Well, it's a pretty simple layout. There are three buildings. The main building is the largest. That building takes care of all of the finances and everyday expenditures of the labs. The two smaller buildings are mainly offices of the lab workers. Now, as we know, along with the three buildings there are three sublevels that are interconnected by a tunnel system. This is where the labs are. The first two sublevels' research tends to be on the up and up as far as I can tell. But, the third sublevel I have nothing on. I don't mean just nothing, but I could only find one set of blueprints that said the damn thing even existed. Brent and Theo could tell you more about the security," Gen remarked, looking over at Brent.

"Well," Brent put in around a bite of cereal. *Wait, when did he get that?* I shook my head and tried to listen. "Luckily, when they hired the new security team about three months ago, I just happened to get a position as an IT tech with them. Funny how that works." He winked at Gen, of all people. "But, even with me being on the inside it isn't going to be a walk in the park. This security team, Branson Security, is made of former military and special ops personnel. In short, they aren't fucking around. There are cameras everywhere leading up to the third sublevel. Then they bring out the big guns: fingerprint scanners, thermal camera, key card entry only, the works."

"Well, it's not all bad. If we can get someone through the first checkpoint we have a better chance," Theo said, pointing to the map. "Here, in the main building. Every employee must check in with one ID card. Then they must go to their office to retrieve a second card that will allow them to enter to their highest level of clearance. The biggest issue is getting someone in. While guests are allowed past the first level, they aren't permitted past that. Take the elevator, for instance. While the thermal cameras are easy to get around, there is a fingerprint pad that allows only people with clearance to the sublevels."

"Well, what about the fingerprint scanners and video feed? I mean, how do we fake that?" I asked. I could drop a man twice my size, but technology more complicated than my iPhone and laptop? Forget it, I'm a certifiable moron.

Brent gave me an, *Oh, you poor little dummy,* smile and said, "Video is the easiest to get around and fingerprints are doable. I have been working for them for two months now. The hard part is getting past the second security check point. The one past the cameras and fingerprints. We can't make a copy of the ID swipe card; the mechanism that reads the cards is too sensitive for that. We have to have the real thing. It's state of the art. It's quite ingenious how the whole ID card reader works. First, the magn ..."

"Brent, buddy," Lachlan blessedly cut him off. Brent's face went from excited to dashed in that very moment. Poor guy really had a hard-on for this kind of thing. But, I was glad Lachlan stopped him, as my eyes would have glazed over.

"So, if one of these cards goes missing, won't that raise alarm bells?" I questioned. It was one thing to steal this card, but when the person whom the card belongs to found out, the cavalry would be called and our collective asses would be grass. I looked over to Brent and he was chewing on his bottom lip as though he had more to say, yet he remained quiet.

"Not if we take the card and go in that night,"

Lachlan stated with confidence.

"Wait, boss." Theo's voice rang through the room. "This security team has no less than five people on guard there at night. They are only allowed in the main lobby. We will have to deal with them first and they have to check in to the video monitoring station back at their office every hour and a half. So, that gives you one hour to get in and out."

I could never be a thief. I mean, my mind wouldn't have even thought there would be people there, much less what to do if there were.

"Oh, Theo, I have an idea I think you will love," Gen murmured in a husky tone. I raised an eyebrow, but she only eyed Theo.

I looked at Lachlan. His full lips were pursed together in a white line. He wasn't thinking of killing them, was he? No. He wouldn't. I hoped.

"Well, how do we get the card? I mean, I'm fast. I could run in, but locked doors hurt when I run into them. I would have to be let in."

"Just use what's between your legs and I bet Jack will let you right in." Gen's words had such a bite that they lashed at my skin.

"No!" Lachlan bellowed before I had time to say anything.

"Oh, for fuck's sake, Lachlan, that's why she's here. She's cute and pretty. Let her romance her way in," Gen said, annoyed.

The thought of having to play nice and grind on Jack made my stomach turn and I felt bile rise up. I looked up to see Lachlan eyeing me with concern.

"You okay?" Lachlan asked in my head.

"I'm fine."

"I was doing some background on dear Jack," Theo said, looking at me with regret. Regret? I stared at him, confused. "Lachlan was right in saying the team wasn't ready. I hadn't completed his background check. I am so sorry I let you go in there. I'm glad nothing happened. But, I should have said no."

"Spit it out," I urged. There was something he wasn't telling me.

"Jack has two priors that were so buried I had to get a snow plow out to dig them up."

I was holding my breath. I knew what he was going to say before he said it. I was such a moron.

"He had two priors for sexual assault. It looks like he paid the victims off and the company paid to have the files buried under sixteen tons of bullshit."

I should have thought to look into his background; knowing his day-to-day routine wasn't enough. But, I wanted Lachlan to see me as an asset, not a liability. Surely, I was proving the latter to be true.

"I'm sorry," I replied, looking at Theo. I put his ass on the line. Even my pitiful 'I'm sorry' felt trite. "To all of you. I should have waited. Things could have turned out much worse. I'm sorry." I couldn't meet Lachlan's eyes. I didn't want him to see just how much this had rattled me.

"She's not going in there," Lachlan responded, shocking me out of my own head.

Gen and I looked at him in surprise. Gen looked to me and looked me up and down, then her eyes narrowed. *Whoa there, killer, this was not my fault.*

"It will be easy. I have a plan!" I smiled, because the plan I had would be the most awesome payback on the planet.

"Remind me not to get on your bad side, because even that look is enough to know whatever this plan is, it's bad." Theo laughed. Oh, he should be worried.

"Do you think i'm a moron?" Lachlan asked, not leaving my apartment. Everyone else left, you know, like a visitor normally does when it's time to go. But, oh no, not Lachlan. I was starting to wonder if he should be paying rent with how much he was here. I rested my forehead against the door and took a deep breath. I was so sick of fighting with this man at every turn. I turned slowly to face him.

"Damn it, Lachlan. I don't want to fight with you. No, I don't think you're a moron. I just had a plan and I think it will work, but …" He held his hand up to me as a silent request.

"That's not what I am talking about. The plan is fine." He still looked pissed off. Great, something else to be pissed off at me about.

"You. Lied." His words were calm and even, not shaking with anger but stated as a fact.

"What? When did I lie?" I wracked my brain trying to think of everything I told him over the past day and what I lied about.

"You said nothing else happened while you were in the house with Jack. Addison, I can tell when you're lying, and I know you are." My heart sank. I really did not want to have this conversation right now.

"Look, it's been a shitty day. My emotions are a complete mess and frankly, I just want to go to bed and forget everything." I tried to push past him, but he pulled me to his chest.

"Addison, you make me feel things I haven't felt since I was human. Frankly, that scares the shit out of me and even the fear is strange. Addison, let me in." His voice actually shook and it made me look at him in a new way. He looked, well, vulnerable.

"He got grabby with me and forceful. It took me back. I mean, I handled it. He already had the drug you gave me in his system so he was easy to shrug off." I didn't want to talk about more. He didn't need to know about my past. Then he would see me how I saw me. Dirty and all used up.

"It took you back where?" His voice was even and calm. Calm? Ha! What a laughable adjective. He was calm, while I was a complete mess inside. There was a shit storm of old abhorrent memories and wild emotions. My heart was racing and my mind was drowning. Tears pricked my eyes, but I refused to cry. I just wouldn't.

"I-I-I can't." It came out a whisper. *Shit, I can't control anything.* Even if I wanted to tell him, I didn't think there would be any way for me to make a coherent sentence.

"If you want to tell me, I will listen. And when words fail …" He put a hand on either side of my head and looked through my eyes, past the muscle, past the tendons and flesh, past the bone right to my soul. I sucked in a deep breath and closed my eyes. Would I tell him? Should I? Could I? I was conflicted. I had never told anyone about my past. The one time I tried, I got slapped in the face and kicked out.

Mentally I asked him, "How?" It was all my scattered brain could come up with.

"Just like when you speak to me like this. You feel me here. But send me images or whatever you want to show me."

I took a deep breath. Where do I start? Do I show him everything? I started where most things start, at the beginning.

My earliest memories of my mother had to have been when I was three or so. I sent him the image of me sitting on the floor with nothing on but pink panties. I was covered in filth and dirt. I had been playing with Play-Doh and got some of the red clay in my hair. I looked over to my mom, who was passed out on the couch. She was surrounded by empty gin and vodka bottles. I remember walking over to her and poking her nose. She didn't even stir. Her egg-colored hair was matted to her skull. The bits of hair that weren't plastered to her with sweat and dirt spilled down the edge of the couch. There was nothing special about this memory, but I picked this one because it was the moment I gave up on my mom.

I showed him images of Aaron. My brother looked a lot like me, with blond hair and blue eyes. He was seven years older than me and did his best to parent me. I showed Lachlan how he would tuck me in at night, how Aaron would feed me and bathe me. Then I showed him how our mom's boyfriends would beat him for no reason at all.

I flipped to memories of all the men she brought back to the house. There were too many to count. But, to her credit, she protected me from them and when she failed, Aaron did. In fact, that was how she got arrested. A man she brought back was a little too interested in playing with me, got rather intense, and she knocked his block off. That was when I was taken away. I was taken away from my mother who was too drunk most of the time to care about me, but the biggest hurt came when Aaron and I were ripped from each other. He was my protector and my hero. I have not seen him since that day. I was so little I had no way of staying in touch. Every time I went looking for him, all I ever found was his name mentioned in an arrest, then nothing.

I sent him my memories of the different foster homes. The first few didn't work out because of my poor attitude, as they called it. Then, there was the one when I was about six where I was beaten for every mistake, every time I broke a rule, or simply because they were bored. I was at that foster home the longest, for four years. Then, when I was ten, the social workers found my aunt. They told me they were excited because someone wanted me. I showed Lachlan the moment I felt wanted. How my face looked and how my heart felt.

I sent him the memories of my early months there. How happy I was. I had a family and people who loved me. I finally thought I was worth loving. Then I sent him everything else, flooding him with memories of the abuse I suffered for nearly five years. I showed him the moment I gave up on myself. The moment I knew I was worth nothing. The moment I grew up. The moment I told my aunt about the abuse and the moment I was slapped in the face for doing so.

I sent him the memories of my first time trying drugs and the first time trying my drug of choice, heroin. The rush of the first high and feeling of complete control without actually having any. I sent him the burn I still felt, the need I could still taste. I sent him everything. The last thing I sent him was of me standing in front of mirror. This was just after he and I had slept together. It was how I saw myself. I didn't know why I sent him that last image, but it was out of my control at that point.

I opened my eyes to see that we were sitting on the floor. I was on his lap. He opened his eyes to look at me. Did he think I was dirty now too? Christ, I was twenty-five, but in so many ways I was that tear-streaked girl of fifteen. His hand shifted to my cheeks and he wiped away tears. *Had I been crying?* I was open to him, a book he had now read. My pages were torn and jagged. I was raw. Every nerve ending was exposed to him.

"Addison, I …" He paused. I knew what he was going to say. Surely after everything he saw he would want nothing to do with me. Hell, I wanted nothing to do with me, but I really didn't have much choice. "I had no idea someone could go through what you have and come out alive on the other side. That last image, the one of you in the mirror, is that how you see yourself?"

A fresh, hot tear spilled down my cheek. Lachlan swiped it away. I put on a rough and tough front, but the reality of the situation was that I was a quivering, self-loathing mess. I nodded at him; it was all I could manage. I feared if I spoke at that moment, the dam I had erected so long ago would break and I wouldn't be able to hold anything back from this man.

"Close your eyes," he requested as he rested his forehead against mine. I did.

I was washed in memories that weren't mine, a rolodex being spun at top speed until the memory he wanted was found. It was me. Well, it was the first time he saw me. And I was radiant. Truly glowing. Even when I tackled him, I was glowing with this luminescent beauty. There was no dirt or grime covering me. My edges weren't torn or worn. I was whole and beautiful.

The memory faded and I stood in front of him, nude. I tried to pull away from the memory, feeling much like a voyeur, but, he pushed the memory harder. I again looked beautiful. I had a sleek body, toned from the martial arts. Yet, it wasn't my body he focused on; it was my gaze and how I looked at him with sensuality and longing. His mental connection pulled back and I slowly opened my eyes.

"Addison." He said my name with benediction, like a prayer. Never had I heard my name said in such a way. His face was soft with understanding. Then, in his eyes, I saw it. Reverence. The same reverence and benediction as when he said my name. That had been how he saw me from the first moment and even how he saw me now.

"Lachlan." My throat was tight and it came out garbled. But, just like I knew it would, with that one word the dam broke and the flood began.

Thirteen

TWO DAYS WE SPENT IRONING OUT THE PLANS for this job. I was a nervous wreck as I went over everything I was tasked to do. Go in and do my speedy thing, get the card, grab the team and get inside, grab what we needed, race out, and go find a chimichanga. Okay, maybe not that last bit, but a girl could hope, right? I was ready; I needed this job to be done. I needed things with Lachlan to be ironed out. Hell, I really had no idea what was going on. Oh, and then there were the small issues of Cannon and Merriam.

I placed my head in my hands and pressed my palms into my eyes. How does this crap keep finding me? I mean, my luck can't be that bad, can it? And now there I sat in my freaking apartment letting a Vampire dress me. Gen sat just outside my room. Just me and her. Maybe we could paint each other's toenails and reminisce about our school years when I was a cheerleader and she was a band geek. I rolled my eyes at my own silliness. It was just, there was only so much pressure a person could be under before they would snap, and I was fast approaching that limit.

"Let's go, short stuff," Gen called from the other room. I groaned in response. "Quit your belly aching and try on the damn clothes." She apparently heard my groan, which only caused me to groan yet louder.

I opened my eyes and stared at the outfit Gen bought for me to distract Jack. The top was, in true Gen fashion, white leather with intricate beading all over it. Oh, did I forget to mention it was a corset? I think she did it to get back at me. The skirt was high-waisted, teal, chiffon, and flowed to mid-thigh. My eyes slid from the too-revealing outfit to the nude heels that lay just under the punching bag.

I heard Gen's voice call from the living room, "You have to wear heels. And they have to be nude. Trust me, the only thing he will be thinking of is sleeping with you. I still can't believe you only own two pairs of heels." I swear to God all of these Vampires had to have ESP or something. I groaned. I did not want to wear heels.

"Do you know how hard it is to run in heels?" I called back.

I stripped and put the new clothes on. The colors were very pretty, and everything fit well. I looked up to see the full view.

"Gen, I-I, there is no way I can wear this," I very nearly cried, looking at myself in the mirror that hung on my closet door. The skirt was actually a scant higher than mid-thigh and the corset and skirt were about two inches from meeting. If I bent over, the whole world would see what I really had to offer.

"Oh, for the love of all that is holy, just get out here and let me see."

"Ugh, Gen! Isn't that like blasphemy or something? Considering?" I walked out over to the punching bag and slipped on the nude platform heels. I took a deep breath and walk out into the living room, bracing myself for the snickers and snorts of laughter.

Gen sat completely unmoving, in that way Vampires who don't need to breathe or twitch had. My mouth went dry at the expression she had on her face. It was hunger, but at the same time, there was a spark of disappointment. She stood up and walked over to me. Well, walked may be too benign a word. She more stalked over, her motions were so fluid.

She walked a slow circle around me. Goose flesh broke out all over my body under the intensity of her gaze. I had no idea what she was thinking or feeling, but it was unnerving, to say the least.

"W-well?" It was a whisper. Damn, but she was throwing off some mad vibes right now.

"I didn't see it before," she said huskily.

"S-see what?" A shiver wracked through me, causing me to stutter. *Damn it, Addison, get it together.*

"Why Lachlan has been a goddamned fool around you." She stopped in front of me and her gaze never wavered. She was a beautiful woman, and I hadn't realized it until this moment, but there was a vulnerability that lay just past her gaze. And that mere fact softened my emotions toward her. She reached out and tucked a loose curl behind my ear, letting a finger trail from my ear down my neck and rest at my pulse. Which, I noticed, was beating considerably faster than it should.

I started to say something when her pink tongue licked her lips in a slow, wet caress. She leaned close to my neck and I felt her lips brush my throat in a soft kiss. My heartbeat had to be nearing, "You should be in the cardiac unit" levels. Then, just as I gathered enough resolve to tell her I just did not feel that way about her, she licked me. No bite, no sucking, not even a nip. Just a quick, wet lick.

A shiver went through me. I had never felt anything for another woman, but Gen definitely was turning on the, "You might want to think twice about your sexuality" vibe.

Finally, blessedly, I was able to mutter, "Gen, what …" I couldn't finish the sentence with her this close to me. I didn't want to hurt her. I didn't really care for her, but we had finally had this moment and I didn't want to lose it by hurting her. She smiled and dropped her hand from me and stepped back.

"It's okay," she remarked, turning her back to me. Then, in a low tone not meant for me, I thought I heard, "I only wanted to taste you. I think I'm hungry." I frowned. I wasn't attracted to her, only Lachlan, but now I felt something that I didn't know how to name. Something I felt deep in my bones. This wasn't a come-on, but I didn't know what to call what just happened between us.

Gen confused me. I thought this whole time she had a thing for Lachlan, but now I wasn't so sure.

"Gen," I started, but she raised a hand as though she wanted me to stop.

"Lachlan is here. This was less painful than any of our other encounters. You're not as bad as I thought. But, this was nothing. Like I said, I am hungry and should have eaten before I came over." She stalked to the door. Lachlan was here? I didn't hear him. Dang, Vampires and their abilities. I mentally laughed at how silly that statement was coming from me.

Without another word, she left. I had no idea what to say to save the situation, so I just stood there and said nothing. What else could I have done? I was walking to the bedroom when the front door opened and Lachlan walked in. I turned to face him. His permanent five o'clock shadow intensified how gorgeous he was. He wore his usual black leather pants and white T-shirt. I wondered if he owned anything else, even as my mouth watered at the sight of him. Despite it all, I wanted him. I let my eyes slowly travel up him until I met his gaze.

He looked furious. Incensed even. I gasped at the sight of him. What the crap had I done now?

"What? Did I do something wrong?" Then I realized he was looking at all of me. I looked down.

"There is no way you're going out like that. You're a wet dream on heels." He ground the words out between clenched teeth. Christ, did I normally look like a bridge troll?

"Lachlan, that's the point," I tried to explain, putting my hands on my hips and sticking a hip out. He narrowed his eyes at me.

"Like hell, I'm going to let you go anywhere like that." His voice was smooth and firm.

I narrowed my eyes at him this time. I was so done with this push and pull.

"Lachlan, I am glad you think Gen did a good job shopping. But, you know this is just a job right?" I didn't know why he was so pissed, but I was over it. "Why are you so mad at me?"

At that, his face softened and he walked over to me.

"It's not that, Addison. It's knowing how this slime ball will be touching you and thinking about you. It's that this will be over tomorrow and then there is Cannon to deal with. Whatever this is will be over."

I scowled at him and closed what little distance there was between us. I reached up and touched his face. He had such a pained expression that it hurt my heart. "I have no idea what the future holds, but damn, Lachlan, I didn't know you gave up so fast."

A look laced with incredulity flashed over his face. Then he smiled a genuine smile and bent down to kiss me. My eyes fluttered shut and I opened my mouth to him. He lifted me up and I wrapped my legs around his waist, allowing him to carry me to the bed that, thank goodness, was down, and he plopped me into it.

I meant it; I would not give up so easy. I had no clue what the future held for us, but I wasn't willing to go quietly into that good night. I was stubborn, unwilling to just roll over and die. No matter what, I would fight for this.

Did I love him? It was a fleeting question as I felt his tongue circling the pulse at my throat. Heat spiked down my body in a liquid rush and I began to grow wet, readying for him. He took short little nips, never breaking the skin, and I thrust my pelvis up to him, aching for his touch. Questions and concerns may have swirled in my head, but there was one thing I was one hundred percent sure about: our bodies worked. Our bodies needed one another. If everything were as simple for us as this was, then we would know everything.

I belatedly realized that he was no longer kissing and nipping at me. No, he was staring at me, trying to gauge my expression.

"What?" I asked. His face was concerned.

"Where were you just then? You were here, but a million miles away." He rolled off to lay next to me.

"You know how every superhero has a fatal flaw? Well, I think mine is overthinking things." I raised a hand to his face and stroked it. He rolled back on top of me.

"Well, my Wonder Woman, I have just the thing to bring you to your knees." He gave me a wicked grin. His Wonder Woman. Why did my heart do a little flip-flop at the thought of being his?

He slowly pushed my skirt up, revealing myself to him. He licked his bottom lip, causing me to groan, just as his hand brushed the inside of my thigh and rekindled the dull aching throb between my legs. At that cool touch, my legs fell open in supplication. His finger brushed my sex and I tried but failed to stifle a whimper. He paused. In that moment I could not, for the life of me, stop myself from arching up to find his touch.

"You better wear panties when you see him. Because, Addison, this," he slipped a finger along my slick folds "is mine."

His voice was guttural. I looked up to find his eyes were so ice blue they were nearly white. His eyes and tone should have sent me tail tucked to the other side of the planet, but God help me I only seemed to grow wetter for him. I tried to speak, but as I did, he slipped one of his expert fingers inside me. My eyes slid shut and I went completely blank of all thoughts. All except for him.

"Look at you. You're so ready and wet for me. I'm going to lap you all up and then start over," he moaned as he slipped a second finger inside of me. I whimpered under his wicked fingers and felt myself beginning to pant softly. I opened my eyes and looked down at him. In this moment, I knew I would be wrecked for anyone else. This man, he would ruin me. But, oh God, it would be so good.

I closed my eyes and gave myself over to him. Because, hell, there was nothing else to be done.

Fourteen

"I LOOK LIKE A HOOKER," I DECLARED, STARING into the mirror. Gen had just finished adding the last finishing touches on my makeup. I gaped at the reflection staring back at me. I have never considered myself a slouch when it came to makeup, but clearly I was a novice compared to Gen.

My blue eyes sparked with a black to teal ombre effect she somehow managed on my eyelids. My already-full lashes now seemed a mile long. I have only ever been a Chap Stick or clear lip gloss kind of girl, but my lips were currently shellacked with a color called Star Fire Ruby. When I questioned Gen about the need of such a flashy color, her response was insightful to say the least.

In a tone that said just how moronic she thought I was, she stated, "Because, when he sees your ruby lips like this he will think of how those lips will look wrapped around his cock. That's all any man will be thinking about when they see you." I opened my mouth for a retort, but it died on my ruby lips when she scoffed and continued, "Isn't that the point?"

"Come on! Let us see!" Theo called from the living room.

"Fine, but I swear if y'all make fun of me, I'll slash your tires before you have time to stuff another doughnut in your pie holes!"

I took a deep breath and readied myself to face the firing squad. Theo, Brent and Lachlan hovered over papers that were strewn about my living room. Today was the day. I would work my magic on Jack, then we would break into the place, get out, and get chimichangas. It's all about positive thinking, right?

They didn't notice me at first, so I coughed. Brent looked up mid-bite of burrito and his jaw slackened, causing a single black bean to fall from his mouth to the papers below.

"Damn it, Brent, this is why you can't get a date," Lachlan growled. Brent never took his eyes off me. They swept over my body and they stuck on my lips. *Damn, Gen, you may have something here,* I thought. Then Theo looked up. His gaze raked my body, only pausing at my breasts, then he too stopped at my lips. Both men gaped at me with expressions that could only be described as dumbfounded. I'd always thought I was cute, maybe even pretty. But, at this moment I felt desired, and it felt good.

Lachlan looked to the two men, then at me. His eyes widened, traveling the length of my body for only a moment, then he too stopped at my lips. But, his was a look of knowing. He knew what it felt like to have my lips wrapped around ... okay, time to think about something else.

I felt kind of silly just standing there with all three men staring at me. I looked at the doorway to my bedroom and saw Gen leaning against the door frame. Her arms were crossed and she raised her brows at the guys, rolling her eyes at them.

She mumbled something that sounded something like, "Stupid men," just before she turned away.

I cleared my throat and asked, "Well, I guess that means it looks okay?"

Theo shook his head and murmured in a low, husky tone, "Honey, you don't look like a hooker, you look like a damn erotic fantasy."

Then, Lachlan stood up and walked over to me. Never taking his eyes off me, he called over his shoulder, "Get back to work."

In my mind, I heard his throaty voice, "I have half a mind to bend you over that couch and take you right the fuck now."

My cheeks flushed and my blood rushed to heat my sex. Christ, I hated how this man seemed to have a direct line to my panties ... well, if I were wearing any. My eyes raked his chiseled body, taking in every bulging muscle and taut line until I came to the impossibly large one in his pants. Clearly, someone was happy to see me.

He stopped right in front of me and put a finger

under my chin tearing my eyes away from the prize that lay in his pants. He kissed me. It was a kiss that was laced with passion, but overwhelmingly so with possession.

He pulled away and mentally agreed, "Gen is right. All I could think about when I saw your lips was how they would look wrapped around my shaft."

My jaw hit the floor and my cheeks flamed.

My eyes slid from Lachlan to Brent, who was looking at me as though he was desperate to speak to me. I pursed my lips and said, "Brent, I need help with something in my car. Will you help me?"

He smiled and stood up, brushing his pants free of any stray burrito. Lachlan eyed me and I gave him a, *"Don't worry about it"* expression, then walked out of the apartment with Brent trailing my heels like a puppy.

I turned and he about barreled into me before catching himself at the last second.

"What, Brent?" It came out much shorter than I intended.

"The night you followed me when I, um, saw Gen. Well, I wasn't there just to be her donor. Since you don't know her, you wouldn't know, but something has been going on with her. Since you joined she had closed herself off. So, I did some digging. I stumbled on a bank account. It's one that is off-shore. There have been three major deposits in the last three months." For once Brent's voice was firm and unwavering.

"So, what if she's moving her money around? Brent,

I don't see how …" I trailed off at the look of pain that flashed across his face.

He shook his head and said, "No, two were from a ghost. An account I couldn't track. But, one …" He met my eyes and they glistened with unshed tears. "The last one led back to Branson Security." It was like a physical blow that sent the breath from my body. Shit, now what do I do?

"Why tell me and not Lachlan?" I questioned.

"Because I don't want her hurt. I-I-I love her. And I know if I tell him, he will likely deal with her." His face was grave and I knew he was right. But, what the hell did he expect me to do? Just as I was about to ask him for his proof, I heard Lachlan's voice in my head.

"Get up here."

With that we both walked up the stairs. I had this awful feeling of foreboding. Now, I didn't know who I could trust. When I walked through the door, Gen was standing at the doorway to the bedroom. I eyed her, trying to see any hint of deception. Not really sure what I thought I would see but I just saw her calm, unmoving expression.

Lachlan walked over with a questioning expression on his face. I just smiled at him and mentally added, "Not now."

"Gen, you and Addison need to go. It's time," Lachlan announced, never taking his eyes off me.

We talked about how much backup I needed and who it should be, and in the end we settled on Gen, as she knew the compound like the back of her hand.

The only issue was it would be high noon and, hello, she was a Vampire. Though she could withstand some sun, she couldn't be bathed in it. When I questioned her about the logistics of this, she told me not to worry about it, that she had SPF 6,000. Plus the car we were taking had windows that were tinted within an inch of their lives.

I had such a bad feeling about this whole thing. I mean, good grief, I teach martial arts; I am no actress, nor am I a thief. I must have had a panicked look on my face, because I felt Lachlan's strong hands delicately cradle my face.

"We have been over this four hundred times. In and out, Addison. Slip him your special little pill then get the fuck out of there. This will be easy; you got this."

I nodded.

"I have your bag. Let's do this," Gen said, opening the door. I followed her out. I didn't look back. This would be easy, right? Because everything I do is. I groaned and got into the car.

"Special pill, check. Fake ID card, check. Mace tucked in my bag, check. Am I forgetting anything?" I asked, trying to hide the small tremor I had developed the closer we got to our destination.

"Head out of your ass?" Gen replied in a snippy tone.

"Nope, it's too far up there. I am now wearing my ass as a hat," I replied back in the same tone. I reached for the handle, but Gen leaned across me and grabbed my hand.

"How do you call me if you need help?"

"Press the button on my ring." Gen had given me a turquoise ring that was actually a small button. It would alert her that I needed her to come save my ass. When I asked her if it was some kind of satellite technology she laughed and quipped, "It's one of those old lady buttons that people have for when they break a hip. You know, 'Help, I've fallen and can't get up.'" I rolled my eyes, but went with it anyway. Talk about the most up-to-date technology, sheesh.

She released the handle and I eased out of the car, taking a deep breath before walking toward the main entrance of the compound. *Fake it till you make it, right? Well, let it happen, captain.* Just before I left, I glanced at Gen, taking a second to see if there was any deception in her gaze. I saw nothing, just intensity for the job she would be performing. I was not cut out for this 'who is betraying whom' bullshit.

I planned this so that when I walked in the front door, Jack should be returning from lunch three or four minutes behind me. If this worked, he would be taking me to his main office. Then, I would do my thing.

The main building was state-of-the-art in every sense of the word. Clearly, this company was way in the black, with its black-and-white marble covering the floor, dark furniture and frosted-glass accents. The place was spotless. There were security guards and people in business attire scattered throughout the lobby, and I turned more than a few of their heads.

I had to fight from blushing or running in the other direction, instead sauntering up to the lobby desk, where a young man in a gray tailored suit stood. He had a wicked little smile that read, "I could give you a good time." He was young, with short-cropped brown hair with more length on top. I had no idea what the style was called; he was clearly trying for David Beckham, but was achieving the look of the soccer ball instead. But, hey, who was I to judge?

"He-llo," the young man seemed to draw the word out.

"Hi! I was wondering if Jack Tellman is here."

His eyebrows shot up in surprise. His stare looked me over as though he could not believe I was here for Jack.

"Uh. Um. He is, let me check his office. Are you sure you're here to see him?"

It took everything in me not to make some kind of pithy retort. But, I smiled and tilted my head and exclaimed, "Gosh, I think so!"

"Addy?" I heard Jack's voice right on cue. I turned to see his eyes hovering in the area of where my ass was. I smiled mentally, making a note to thank Theo for the training on tailing people.

"Jack!" He had his lab coat on, along with a fitted blue-and-white pinstripe shirt and a black tie. If I didn't know he were a sexual predator and downright asshole, I would say he looked handsome. Alas, I forced a smile and walked over to him, turning my flirt dial up to an eight by throwing my arms around him and hugging him. His body went rigid under the embrace.

I leaned in close to his ear and whispered, "I had to see you again. I couldn't stop thinking about you." I felt him harden against me as I pressed tightly to him.

"Hi, Addy! I didn't think you wanted to see me again after I passed out. I don't even remember much about that night. Wow, you look," he ran a hand over his mouth and in a gruff tone he finished, "good enough to eat."

I smiled and batted my eyes at him. "You're so sweet. I am sorry to just show up, but I didn't have your number and I remembered you worked here. This place is amazing! I'll understand if you want me to go."

His eyes flicked to my lips. I snaked my tongue out to brush my bottom lip and I saw him shudder at the gesture.

"No!" The word seemed to surprise him with the force at which it came out. "I mean no, let me give you a tour and show you my office. Also, I had your blood analyzed, and I would love to share with you what I found." Shit, I had forgotten all about the blood he had taken, but I was honestly intrigued by this admission.

"Lead the way," I said.

Just to enter into the main building I had to leave my ID, which was fake, a credit card, also fake, and fingerprints. Now, I couldn't fake those, but Brent assured me he would work his "geek hojo mojo." Whatever that meant.

Once in the elevator, Jack turned to me, putting a

hand on either side of my head. He pressed his body against me and I felt his desire for me against my belly. I stifled a shudder of disgust.

"I am shocked to see you, Addy. Glad, but shocked," he said as he leaned his head to my hair. He took a deep breath and I felt him press more firmly into me.

"Well, I remember you telling me about your office and, well, I have this little fantasy," I responded shyly.

"Oh, what's that?"

"To be bent over a desk." I arched myself toward him. His eyes seemed to smolder with need. I must be good.

With that, the door dinged and he turned and pulled me by my arm down the hallway. All of the frosted-glass doors were shut. Everything about this building screamed money, from the fixtures to the accents. His office was on the left at the end of the hallway and he nearly ripped my arm off to get to it. This hallway was long, as it was the main connection to the other smaller building where the lab employees' offices were.

"Addison?" I froze at the male who just called my name. *Fuck! Who the hell could know me here?* I turned to see Kyle's frowning face looking back at me. *This shit just keeps getting better and better.*

I KNEW THE SHOCK SHOWED ON MY FACE BECAUSE they both just stared at me. I was going through a thousand things that could possibly happen while I was here and this wasn't even on the same planet of possibilities. Fuck me!

"Kyle, hi, I had no idea you worked here." He frowned at me, and I realized he might have told me at some point and I likely just tuned him out. *Good fucking job, Addison.*

"Yeah, I just started. I work in the accounting department." His eyes flicked from me to Jack, who eyed him with increasing interest. I looked at Kyle and then realized what I had to do.

He was staring at me like he was about to ask a question; any question would surely lead to more and I really needed to nip this now before the shit hit the proverbial fan, so I stiffened my spine and said, "Wow, Kyle, that's great, but Jack and I have some business to take care of." I turned to walk away when I heard Kyle's voice.

"The same kind of business I walked in on a few weeks ago? You sure do bounce from one guy to the next." The words seemed to echo off the walls of the hallway. They slammed into me, nearly knocking the breath right out of me. I had no intention of hurting him; all I wanted to do was to brush him off, but now, now I was ticked.

Jack looked from me to him, then his eyes narrowed. I had to save this situation, but I was in shock. I would never expect something so hateful to come out of his mouth. I glanced up at Jack and smiled.

"I have this," I replied, then turned to face Kyle.

I took a deep breath, because I knew I would have to hurt him even further.

"Kyle, honey, did you really think it would work? You were less than vanilla. You want to know what I thought about when I was with you? Fucking someone else, anyone else. You were so boring," I revealed in my best *"I couldn't care less about you"* tone.

His stony face faltered, showing just how much my words hurt. My heart was breaking because I did like Kyle, just not in the way he wanted me to. I could see him working up the nerve to respond, so in my harshest tone I added, "I moved on to better and much bigger things. So, why don't you go calculate something?"

Without a look over my shoulder, I turned and looked at Jack, whose jaw was a mere inch from hitting the floor.

"Let's go, I'm done here."

Jack paused for only a moment before we continued on to his office. My heart broke for what I had just said to Kyle. I had to make it right with him when this was done. I don't know how, but I would. For now, I injected what little steel I could muster into my spine and walked to Jack's office.

The moment I stepped in, I had no time to even survey my surroundings. He pushed me against the door and started kissing my neck.

"Whoa, Jack," was all I could manage before he crushed his lips to mine. My stomach lurched in revulsion, but I had to get through this. He surprisingly broke the kiss and stared down at me.

"God, Addy, the things I am going to do to your little body." His eyes blazed with lust. He ground his pelvis against me again. I maneuvered out from under him and gave him a wicked little smile.

His office was oddly huge, considering how little time he spent in it, according to my observations. A row of cabinets made a shelf along one wall. Glass overlooking the compound made up the back wall, while stunning artwork decorated the others. His L-shaped desk sat toward the glass wall, and was black, much like the rest of the fixtures in the building, leading me to believe that it was company issued.

"I would kill for a cup of coffee," I hinted, walking over to the Keurig machine. I knew he wouldn't say no. The guy lived off this stuff and he always had a cup after lunch before returning to work. I was so glad Lachlan made me watch this guy like a hawk until I could complete his daily routine in my sleep.

"The cups are under the machine. Make me one as well. I will pull out your blood work," he replied, walking over to his desk. I slowly bent over, giving him a view of my bared ass. He groaned, "Christ, Addy, hurry before I bend you over my desk now." I stifled a wretch, but only barely.

I slipped the magic pills into his coffee and hand delivered it to him before I made mine. I smiled at him, knowing just what was about to happen. *I am a sick person.*

"Here you go, honey. I made it just for you." That wasn't a lie. I walked over to the coffee machine and put another K-cup in for my cup of coffee.

One of the things I had learned about Jack in the

last few days was his view of women. He was reported to view them much like a stereotypical chauvinistic man in his forties would. They needed to stay at home and service him. Little did he know, I was not the servicing type.

I walked over and stood by his chair, looking at the papers stacked neatly on his desk.

"So, tell me, Jack. What does my blood tell you?" I asked in a husky tone.

He took a sip of his coffee and raised a hand to my leg, rubbing his hand along the length of my thigh while he spoke. I had to stifle a shiver of disgust.

"Well, missy, I have seen the abnormalities in the DNA of pushers and they are much the same, always located in the same places. But your DNA, it's just so beautiful. Look."

I walked over and peered just over his shoulder. On the screen were bars and numbers that honestly made little sense to me.

"Not to sound uneducated, but what is it that I am looking at?"

He laughed in that patronizing way people did when they thought someone simple or beneath them.

"It's okay, Addy. Not everyone knows what this stuff is." I was one more snide comment away from me jumping on his back and throttling him.

"See these series of markers here? These are mine. See how they are even, and if I were to manipulate them, much like a strand of DNA, they would spiral into the form of DNA I am sure you have seen before."

He then pointed to the other side of the screen with more than twice as many dark bars.

"These are your genetic markers. Addy, you have more than I have seen, even compared to other pushers. Your abnormalities, like other pushers, are on a cellular level, but, Addy, yours are buried so deep within your genetic code that I would be willing to bet that your whole family would be pushers in one form or another."

"Well, I know my brother is a pusher, but I haven't seen him in a number of years." Damn it, despite the job I was here for, I felt like I needed to know more. Talk about a dangerous case of curiosity.

He took a long pull of his coffee and continued. "I would love to meet him and take a sample from him. And, Addy, I am willing to bet if you have children they would have just as many abnormalities as you, if not more."

"What if the father was a non-pusher?" Crap, I knew I was becoming too engrossed with this conversation, but I couldn't help myself.

He shook his head and replied, "That wouldn't matter. Your genetics are so strong that they would overpower any others."

If I wasn't jumping to any conclusions, I gathered that he was calling me the missing link. Holy shit, my genetics could be the start of a more permanent change for the human race?! This revelation both thrilled and scared the hell out of me. There were a lot of factions out there that did not like pushers and were doing everything they could to create a stigma against them.

I looked at Jack, who was still talking and drinking his coffee.

"Addy, the things we could do with your DNA alone." He raised his hand along the back of my thigh and ran it up and down, from my knee to the hem of my rather short skirt. Then I heard a gurgling noise deep within his belly and had to stifle a smile. His eyes went wide.

"Jack, are you okay?" I asked, leaning down to place a kiss upon his neck.

"Yes, of course," he groaned in a pained tone. I pulled my head back to look at him. Sweat had begun to bead on his upper lip and brow.

"Jack, are you sure? You don't look so good," I commented in a worried tone.

I heard a low growl from his stomach and then I heard him squeak one out. I gave him my best horrified look, trying desperately not to break out in giggles. He returned my horrified look in kind.

"Addy, uh, stay here. I'll be right back," he said in a panicked tone. He got up, his butt cheeks so clenched that he basically waddled to the door.

"Please don't touch anything," he added just before he got to the door.

I raised my right hand and held up three fingers and promised, "Scouts honor." And with that, and a surprising amount of speed, he was gone. I then lowered two of the three fingers and smiled at the door.

The laxatives I slipped into his coffee was super-fast acting and fairly long lasting, but I had to hurry.

The damn little pill was the horse tranquilizer of laxatives. I smiled and giggled at the thought of what he was going through as I opened all of his drawers and filed and flipped through the contents of all of them. I found his Checkpoint 2 ID badge in the third drawer and replaced it with an identical one that Brent made. Brent assured me his would not work and they would have to demagnetize it and re-magnetize it and would assume his became demagnetized somehow.

I shoved the ID badge in my bra, then walked over to his computer and hit the 'print screen' key. I knew it was selfish, I knew that I shouldn't have done it, but for crap's sake, I wanted a copy of it. Then I hit delete. It wasn't a surefire way to clean the internet world of my information, but Brent had me covered there.

I walked over to the door and placed my ear against the cool glass. Not hearing anything, I grabbed the papers from the printer and folded them up, then put them in the other cup of my bra. Hey, isn't that what these things were good for? My tiny purse was already full, so it was my only option.

I opened the door and saw Jack walking toward me. His face was so pale it was nearing green. I again had to muffle a laugh. I couldn't help it. Seeing him in anguish over trying not to shit his pants was hilarious.

"Hey, Jack, are you okay?" I asked, sounding concerned.

"No, I think I'm sick. I think I'll have to say good bye. I would walk you out but ..." He trailed off, a sweat beginning to roll from his hairline down his temple. I heard another loud gurgling noise and met his eyes.

"It's okay, I can see myself out. Another time, I suppose."

"Wait, can I get your number?" He essentially yelled the words. He looked like his comfort level was that of someone who took a romantic romp with a cactus. It was only by the grace of God that I didn't break out in giggles at the image.

I took a pen from his jacket and lifted his sweaty palm up, scribbling a number on it. Oh, not my number, but one of my former dealer's numbers. Who happened to work at the Gold Club. I smiled the whole time, trying to not bust out in snorts and fits.

He didn't even wait for me to turn and walk away before he ran in the direction of the assumed bathroom. I smiled and left.

Fifteen

"**W**ELL?" NOT *HI* OR *HELLO* OR *HOW DID IT GO*, but *well*. Ugh.

"Well, Gen, it was fine. I don't know where you got that laxative from, but remind me to never get on your bad side," I laughed, handing her the badge.

"I can't believe you got it!" she replied as she pulled away from the compound. It took an incredible about of self-restraint not to back hand her. She continually had no faith in me, and it pissed me off.

We sat the rest of the way in silence, both trying to mentally prepare for what was about to come. Tonight was the night. We would be going in, getting every bit of the drug, and implanting a computer virus that corrupted anything with numbers in it. Well, that's how I understood how the virus worked. Brent said the virus was pretty simple and worked in two parts. It attacked all existing files and then it worked on email lists. The virus could somehow track the footprints of emails sent out and then could wreak havoc on other computers containing those files.

When I asked about paper files, he scoffed and said that was so Eighteenth Century, but Lachlan assured me that he and Theo had that covered. And, that my whole job was to go in with Lachlan and then get out with any physical remnants of the drug.

When we got back to my apartment, I mentally called to Lachlan right before we got out of the car.

"Hey." With that word to him I could feel his tension lift. I had no idea how I knew I felt that, but I had.

"Did everything go okay?" His mental voice was calm, yet for whatever reason I knew he wasn't. I made a mental note to ask him why I felt these weird feelings.

"Yeah, had a run-in with Kyle of all people, but I have it."

"Good."

Gen and I walked up to my apartment building and I was just about to walk in when she grabbed my upper arm and whirled me to face her.

"What the hell?"

Her eyes were full of concern. "Look, we don't have much time, but this thing you have with Lachlan is going to get him killed. I know nothing I say will sway you, but please stop being selfish and for God's sake think of him. Think of the pain being with you will cause him. And if not pain, certain death. Addison, I know you don't like me, but not even your love for him will be enough to save him from Cannon or Merriam. It will only doom him."

She walked into the building. I was left standing there. She was right, and it hurt so damned badly to admit that. I would bring him nothing but pain. Her words were the cement that placed the last brick on the wall I would have to hide behind. They rang so true. What is that saying? If you love something, you need to set it free? Well, I didn't know if I loved him, but I did care for him and didn't want anything to happen to him.

Tears pricked my eyes and I felt one slip out and run down my cheek. I swiped it away and swallowed the pain that had formed a lump in my throat. Steeling my nerves, I ascended the stairs to finish this.

"DOES EVERYONE KNOW THE PLAN?" LACHLAN EYED each of us in turn. But, when he got to me, he lingered, trying to read my expression. He felt me pull away from him; I made it so he couldn't ask me. I shut him out mentally, saying I wanted to focus on the job. *What a load of crock.*

"Yeah, boss," Theo replied.

"Brent, you have the cameras?"

"Yeah, I have been recording for two months and I have a loop ready. The loop is five hours. But, I would keep this little visit to one hour. Theo and Gen will keep the security guards busy enough, but once you're in, you need to set a timer. The guards must ring the home base every hour and a half per protocol. I will drive over to home base and direct my portion from there." Brent gave his response in a calm tone. How the flying hell was he calm? He was never calm. He resembled a bowl of Jell-O, he trembled so violently. I had such a feeling of unease about this whole damned situation.

"Addison." Lachlan was looking at me with concern in his blue eyes. I blinked rapidly and nodded in question. I couldn't really speak to him or I would confess everything I was feeling, and this really wasn't the time for that.

"Once we get down to the sublevel the lab is on, I am going to need you to do your thing and sprint around until we find where they are keeping this drug."

"Wait. How will we know what drug it is? I mean, I don't think there will be a label on it that says, 'highly unethical and illegal drug' on it." I didn't know why this question just hit me as a possible problem, but it did.

"It will be the only thing on Jack's station. Also, the drug will be kept in safe areas where only his ID card could get into," Theo informed me confidently. I'm glad someone was feeling cocky because that was the last thing I was feeling.

"And we are sure about this?" I had to ask it. I mean, I was putting everything on the line here.

Theo raised his eyebrow at me in incredulity. He then covered his chest just over his heart with his hand and said, "Addison, you wound me. I have done my job, chickadee, now it's your turn."

Crap. He was right. And now I felt like an ass.

"Sorry, I guess I am just nervous," I said, not able to meet Theo's eyes. I felt a warm hand grasp mine and looked over.

Theo held my hand and whispered in a tone only meant for me, "It's okay, chickadee, I still love you. And I got your scrawny ass. Worry not." He squeezed my hand to add more emphasis to his words.

I looked at each person in turn and had to trust that they each held up their end of the bargain. I had to trust that they would not screw this up. And they had to trust me when they had no reason to.

"Okay, let's go." Lachlan's command broke up the moment. He handed each of us a small peach-colored earpiece. "Okay, you will be able to talk with each other with these. I will communicate telepathically with everyone, but these are for you to talk to everyone else." He stuffed the device in his right ear. I did the same.

We were both dressed in black. Gen, however, had on a red leather cat suit and Theo had on jeans and a baggy T-shirt. They would act as a diversion to get the guards away from the front desk long enough for Lachlan and me to make it to the elevators past the first checkpoint.

"Let's do this," Lachlan asserted, opening the door to my apartment.

I looked up to the sky as we walked to the car and said a fast prayer to the benevolent God/goddess/gods or whatever was possibly up there. "Take pity on me will ya? Oh, amen." Then I got into the car.

———————

"I'M SORRY, I SHOULD HAVE ASKED, BUT WHAT IS THE diversion?" I turned to Lachlan as he put the car in park.

"Oh, honey, you'll know it when you hear it," Gen answered, eyeing Theo. And I'll be damned if he didn't blush.

Both Lachlan and I gathered the two backpacks and put them on. Theo and Gen ran to the side of the compound. We parked about a quarter of a mile away from the building, where the security firm parked. We had a good line of sight of the front entrance and Gen assured me that whatever the distraction was, it would send these guys running. Then it was my job to get Lachlan and myself in. I assured her that I could get us in before the front door closed.

I was so glad I had a fresh mental image of the front lobby to the elevator in my head. I closed my eyes and focused on the length of the hallway and how many steps it would take for me to get to every turn. I pictured all of the fixtures and furniture, the first checkpoint ID station. I ran through it for about the hundredth time. All I would need to do was grab Lachlan's arm through mine and pull him with me as I ran.

I switched my focus to the sounds coming from the earpiece, which at this point were difficult to ignore. Was that heavy breathing? And grunting? And smacking? If I didn't know better I would think they were making out. Then I heard a loud moan. Oh, for shit's sake. I flushed. They weren't, were they? I looked over at Lachlan, who had his eyes glued on the front door.

Mentally, I asked, "They aren't, you know? Are they?"

"Yeah, they are. Why, is it turning you on?" Yet more heat rushed to my face.

"No!" I answered a little too quickly. I was horrified to realize that the sounds coming across the earpiece were, in fact, turning me on.

"Go time," he stated.

I pulled the binoculars from his hands and eyed the door. The guards had just reached for the front handle. And, just like Gen assured me, every last one of them was filing out of the damned building. Just as the last one got to the door, I grabbed Lachlan's arm and pulled him along with me. The world melted into blended colors of the night. And, just as I assured Gen, we were in the building before the door closed behind the last guard.

Mentally, Lachlan exclaimed, "Christ, woman. That was the most intense thing I have ever felt!" I caught sight of his eyes as we stood in front of the elevator, flickering from blue to ice in an instant. There were two sets of elevators, and we were ninety percent sure that this was the set that led to the sublevel lab Jack worked in. He pressed the button and the doors opened immediately. *Of course they did.*

We entered the small space and he slipped on a special glove that would get the elevator to the third sublevel. All I was told was these gloves made this part possible. Bret said if he told me how they worked, then he would have to kill me. But they made the first checkpoint possible, so who was I to question?

Lachlan pressed a finger to the small pad and the elevator started to move. Then he pressed the "3SL" button. Through the earpiece I still hear Gen's moans and Theo's grunts. I heard the calls of men telling them to go get a room or they would be forced to call the police, but there was no force behind the threat. Everyone was enjoying the show. I looked over to Lachlan, who was studying me.

"What?" I questioned.

"Why did you shut me out?"

Does he have to ask this now? "Can we talk about this later?" I knew what he would say, but damn it, this was not what I needed right now.

Before he could answer, the door dinged and opened. We stepped out into a hallway. There were double doors about six feet in front of us and I knew this was the second checkpoint. There was a card reader on the wall in front of the right door. I pulled the card out and swiped it. Nothing happened other than a red light turned on. My heart sank. Had I grabbed the wrong one? I could hear the rush of my pulse in my ears. I glanced to Lachlan, who wore a stony expression. He was completely emotionless. I looked back at the card reader and tried again, this time a little slower. The light turned green and the door clicked as it unlocked. Though I knew this was supposed to happen, I stood there staring, dumbfounded.

Lachlan pulled me by the arm and shook me a bit.

Mentally he stated, "It's game time."

I grabbed him and bolted. I ran down hallway after hallway. While I run incredibly fast, my vision keeps up so light and objects don't blur. It's more like the rest of the world slows.

I darted in and out of each room, only pausing long enough to try different card readers. While the information stated that Jack worked on the third sublevel, I was growing panicked because frankly I wasn't finding it. I didn't stop to evaluate each station because we had very little time. But, from the things I did see, this company had more secrets than anything else.

We came to the last station in this building and it was its own lab, locked away behind a door with a card reader. Most of the others were open stations, but this one wasn't. It caused me to pause. I slid the card and heard the door click just as the light turned green. This was Jack's lab.

The lab itself was dark and pristine. There were large tables with expensive equipment placed on them, and refrigerators and cabinets lining three of the four walls. The back wall was bare except for an industrial door and card reader. There were four computers and no less than eight mounted screens.

"Brent, we are in. There are four computers here. Where do I put this nasty USB drive in?"

"Hey, hang on. I have to sift through the cameras

to find you." There was a pause, "Okay, I see you. Put the USB in the one on your far right. But, listen, you need to turn it on and make sure it's connected to the internet first. Then plug it in and download the program. The virus will do the rest from there."

"Got it."

I turned the computer on and waited. Apparently they spent the budget on their new security team, not faster computers. Lachlan was going through all of the cabinets and refrigerators. With each one, he grew more panicked and frustrated. The computer finally finished turning on and it drew my attention away from Lachlan. I checked the internet connection. Everything looked to be in order, so I uploaded the virus. Brent warned me this would take a few minutes, so I walked over to Lachlan.

"Hey, calm down. What's wrong?" I tried to sooth him mentally.

"It's not here. There's nothing. Not one drug in here," he said with an edge.

"Have you tried the door?" I asked calmly. Way more calmly than I felt, that's for sure.

He glanced to it as though he hadn't seen it before.

"No, let's see what's behind door number one, shall we?"

We walked over and I slid the card. But, nothing happened. I frowned at the door and tried again. Still nothing. I looked down at the card reader, hoping it would tell me what I was doing wrong. In green letters it read, "Enter Password."

"Oh shit," I scoffed.

"What?" Lachlan peered over my shoulder.

"Brent, this door requires a password. Can you bypass it?" My heart was pounding.

I heard Theo's voice say, "Our part for now is done. You have thirty minutes max before the secondary diversion to get you out."

Then I heard Brent's voice chime in, "I can get you in the room, but it's going to take a while. And by a while I mean like two hours at the minimum. You'll need to guess it. Try no more than two times, Addison. This system will give you one error and after that it will shut down for an hour." I heard him pounding away on a computer.

"So, two guesses and if I fail then we have to wait an hour," I asked as my heart began to pick up speed.

"Correct. Good luck," Brent replied, still typing away.

This was too much pressure. I walked over to the computer and it read fifty-seven percent complete. Then I walked back to the keypad, leaning against the wall and sliding down it until my ass hit the ground. I pulled my knees up to my chest and set my head on them. My focus was on slowing my breathing and trying to calm down. Who was I kidding? There was no way I could do this.

"Addison." I felt Lachlan's cool touch on top of my head. I raised my head to look at him. His hand moved to the nape of my neck and he seemed to cradle me like that for a long time before speaking.

"Addison, you can do this. You're letting the fear and self-doubt you carry interfere with the reality of the situation."

He was right, damn him. "I just don't want to fail at this." My voice was small and distant.

"I know you don't, but you can't fail or succeed if you don't try."

I hated him for being so damned right.

He pulled me to my feet and into his arms. He angled my head up to his and lightly kissed me. And just like that everything melted away. All of the fear and panic just slid off me. I turned from him to face the keypad. I slid the card and typed in the word: PUSHER. The keypad turned red and read, "Incorrect."

I glanced to Lachlan and took in a deep breath. He wasn't moving, completely still. I closed my eyes and thought back to Jack. Images of him and snippets of conversation flashed in my mind. I plucked one and played it back. It was the image of the sword hanging on his wall. It had been lovingly taken care of and mounted in such a way that took thought, time and money. I replayed the conversation, then opened my eyes and slid the card and typed in the word: KASKARA. I didn't breathe. My heart pounded so hard that I could hear it.

The keypad turned green as the door clicked open.

Sixteen

I'M NOT SURE WHAT I WAS EXPECTING WHEN THE door swung wide, but what I saw wasn't anywhere close to what I thought. It was another room. Another huge, massive room, dark but for hundreds of small red, yellow, and green lights. Lachlan had better night vision than I, so he was looking for a light switch. Without warning he found it and I was temporarily blinded while my eyes adjusted to the new light.

I stood there, blinking at the sight before me. It was like something out of The Twilight Zone. In fact, I wouldn't be at all surprised if the theme song started playing.

There were beds in rows, along the sides of the room. And in the beds were forms that looked an awful lot like people. There had to be over a hundred of them. Any thought of looking for a drug or why I was here slipped away.

I walked over to the first bed on the left-hand side

of the wall. There was, indeed, a man lying in it. He looked to be in his early thirties, with light-brown hair that was beginning to gray on the sides. But he had a very young look to him, and appeared to be sleeping, even though his eyes under his closed lids were darting in every direction. He was hooked up to monitors and tubes, IVs and wires going in just about every direction. The IV bags, however, weren't clear, they were red.

Why were these people here? Were they sick? I just could not comprehend it. There was a metal booklet that sat next to the bed on a small table. I walked over and began flipping through it.

"Seth Growmen. Age: 32 Sex: Male. Ability/ies: Superior Strength. Pusher Rank (1-10): 4. Date Turned: 6/2014. Subject before turning: Subject believed he was attending an interview. He performed a physical where he maxed out his strength by lifting thirteen tons. Once he realized the reality of the situation, he became quite aggressive. He was sedated and turned immediately. Subject after turning: His physical abilities have more than tripled as has his aggression. Sedation should be given by IV every six hours and doubled at night. He is becoming increasingly more tolerant of the medications. I cannot stress enough that the patient is highly aggressive and volatile. May need to be destroyed."

I dropped the metal booklet as though it burned my fingers. I stumbled back and my hand flew to my mouth to stifle a scream. I felt sick. This was a man, a pusher; how could they turn him then speak about killing him so nonchalantly? I couldn't understand it.

I walked over to the next bed. The girl had black hair and looked to be no older than eighteen. Feeling like I was going to throw up, I swallowed hard and picked up her file.

"Lexi Choo. Age 19 Sex: Female Ability/ies: Telepathy Pusher rank (1-10): 3. Date Turned: 2/2015. Subject before turning: Lexie was a runaway whom we pulled off of the street for this trial. She was eager to try anything and put up little fight. Her telepathy was quite impressive and very willing to be turned. Very little aggression shown at this time. Subject after turning: Her aggression level increased tenfold and her ability to read minds transformed to the ability to control people through their minds. When given live food, she proved to be particularly ruthless. She enjoys playing with her food. She could be controlled, though her ability will make it likely that she will turn on her controller. But, in the last few days she has responded to the controllers. This is the breakthrough patient. Do not destroy."

My vision was blurring at the words. I looked down the rows of beds, then to Lachlan, who was placing things from the refrigerators in his bag.

"L-Lachlan," I drawled the word out loud, though it was shaky. I didn't think I could effectively mentally communicate. The words *"May need to be destroyed,"* kept repeating in my mind. Over and over.

He faced me and his eyes went wide at my expression. He walked over and looked down at the form on the bed, then picked up the file and scanned it. His face grew angrier by the moment, his knuckles turning white from his grasp on the file.

"We … we have to get these people out of here, Lachlan." My words sounded small, distant. I was in shock and I knew it. But, I couldn't make myself stiffen up and grow a pair. That ability was gone.

"Addison."

I knew that tone and it seemed to snap me out of this shock I found myself in. "I mean it, Lachlan. I will not leave these people behind." I was firm in this. These were people; no matter what had been done to them, they were people.

"Addison, listen to me. We could not possibly bring them. We don't have the ability."

"Then what do we do with them? Leave them!?" I was yelling and felt tears prick my eyes, but I was resolute in the fact that I would not leave them.

"No, Addison, we are going to do what I have planned to do with the building." His tone was even, as though he knew he would find these people here. That's when it hit me. I took a step back to look at him more fully.

"Oh, my God. You knew they would be here. You knew." I was completely astonished. He hadn't told me. I felt betrayed.

"Addison, please, we need to get out of here. We don't have time for this." He took a step toward me and I stepped back in kind.

"I'm not going anywhere until you explain." I crossed my arms over my chest. I didn't care if I went to jail for it, but I would not leave these people behind.

He ran a hand through his hair and narrowed his eyes at me. Then he sighed, "Fine. Yes, Gen and I knew they were bringing pushers in about two weeks ago. Addison, these aren't people anymore; this must be done." He walked over to my bag and pulled out several blocks of what looked to be tan clay. He ran down the building's expanse, nearly going out of sight. I ran after him as he sporadically placed the small blocks under the every third or so bed. It dawned on me what he had planned.

"So, you're going to kill all of these people?"

He stood up and closed the distance between us. "These," he pointed to the beds, "are not people, Addison. They are monsters."

"Then what does that make you?" I couldn't even breath, I was so incensed. Pain flashed across his face, but it was quickly replaced with firm resolution, a mask of a man both detached from the situation and set on the course of action.

"Addison, please, you don't understand what these things are capable of."

"You do this, Lachlan, and that river of blood that flows behind you will become an ocean." I used his own words with hopes they would cause some kind of emotion. A barely perceptible flinch, but it was there.

He searched my eyes for something. I guess he was looking to see what hung in the balance. And the truth was, everything did.

Then his words hit me like a physical punch. "So be it."

My heart stopped beating at his callous words.

"We need to leave now. I have every last bit of the drug and Brent's virus is doing its thing." He grabbed my arm, but I was unmoving.

"No." I tried to step back from him; his hold was iron.

"Addison, now. I mean ..." His words were cut off by a pop of air and then I felt a sharp sting in my ass, of all places. His eyes went wide.

"I was just stung by a bee," I said, turning around. I felt a tug and then turned to face Lachlan.

He held what looked like a tranquilizer dart. *Oh shit.*

"Run," I ordered, or at least I thought I did. My body began to feel as though I was being buried in sand or mud. Things were going numb and my mind was becoming increasingly fuzzy.

I belatedly realized that I was looking up at Lachlan from a much more severe angle than I had. *I must be laying on the floor.*

I heard a distant voice say, "I'll be back for you. I have to get this drug out of here." Black dots began dancing their way into my vision. Nearly an hour? No, thirty seconds? No, that couldn't be right. Soon, I heard the pitter patter of thousands of feet, or maybe ten; hell, it could have been none. The world narrowed to a small pinpoint and I thought I saw Jack's smiling face, but then my vision went black.

Seventeen

I HEARD THE SLAP BEFORE THE SHARP PAIN registered. Oh shit, I was going to vomit. My stomach was on total revolt. I was slapped again and this time I felt it. I tasted blood, then spat on the floor.

"Oh look, our princess is awake." It took a few long moments for the voice to register. The voice was familiar, but my muddled mind really could not comprehend, much less sift through all of the stimuli I was experiencing. I tried a few times to open my eyes. It felt like my eyelids were sandpaper, but I managed it. And all I was rewarded with was my eyes being assaulted with blinding light.

I tried to play back the last thing I could recall. I was stung by a bee. Wait. No. That wasn't right. I was hit by some kind of dart with drugs in it. Oh fuck, Lachlan. Had he gotten away? Had he left me? No, I couldn't speculate. I attempted opening my eyes; finally

242

they were getting used to the light and I was beginning to make out the form in front of me as a man.

"Don't call me princess." It was little more than a rasp, but hey what can I do.

"Addy. You just look so beautiful tied up like this." Addy. It was Jack. Tied up? I looked down to find that I was zip tied to a metal chair. *Great, just fan-freaking-tastic.*

"I'm going to vomit if you keep complimenting me," I retorted in a cold tone. But, it was true. I felt like I was hit by a Mack Truck and four hundred of his closest trucker buddies. I tried to get my muddled mind to kick it in high gear, but everything was sluggish.

Then I realized I wasn't alone in the room. There were five other men, all dressed in black fatigues. They were all built and overly muscular, with the same buzz cut, though they ranged in height.

"Did your band of merry men plan on wearing the same outfit and haircut? Or was that just a coincidence? Because I'll tell you, it's really cute when couples, even if there are five of you, dress alike."

Jack slapped me again, causing my left cheek to feel as though it were on fire. Again I tasted blood, but instead of spitting, I gave him a pout.

"I've been hit harder by a ten-year-old with a yellow belt."

He moved to hit me again, but I flexed my telekinetic power to stop him. It didn't work. Cold washed over me just before his closed fist hit my jaw. Pain exploded from the blow and my vision blurred.

But, blessedly, he didn't break a bone. No powers, now that made me worry. My heart rate sped up.

Jack must have seen the complete look of panic on my face.

"Addison, your abilities will not do much good right now. The drug you were shot with will stunt your abilities for a few hours."

I relaxed infinitesimally at his words. There was comfort knowing that my abilities would return.

"What do you want, Jack?" My tone was that of someone who was so over this conversation, mainly because I was.

My mind finally registered that I was no longer in the hidden warehouse room with the drugged pushers. I was in a different room. There was nothing in it, not even windows or anything hanging on the walls. Only a wooden door.

"Addison Fitzpatrick. Former drug addict. You have been clean for seven years. You currently work at Darryl's Dojo. You live alone and have no known family other than a mysterious brother. You bounced around from foster home to foster home, then, when you were ten, you we taken in by an aunt and uncle. And this is my favorite part, Addison." My heart stopped with his words.

"Stop." It was a whisper. I did not want to relive this. Not with him. I didn't even like hearing him say my name, much less hearing him retell my life.

"But, Addison, this is my favorite part. I guess we will have to relive that memory when I have you alone."

How had this happened? Brent said he would warn us and he said he had all of the cameras. And how had this guy gotten all of my history? I met his eyes and in them I saw something I couldn't place, so I took a stab in the dark.

"Gen? She was working for you?" That had to be it. I was going to throttle her.

He looked at me with a questioning look. If not Gen, who? Then it clicked. He knew way too much about me. He knew things that I paid people to keep hidden. My heart sank at the thought.

"Brent. He gave someone a file on me, didn't he, and he told you we would be here."

He nodded. "Though the virus was a fun touch. He really did destroy all electronic copies of the drug and your buddy got away with the physical drug. No matter. I have a photographic memory. And paper copies of the most recent breakthrough of the drug. VP673," he stated, tapping his head. "VP673 is perfect. We have about ten pushers who we are now able to control." He looked so smug and proud of himself. I had a vision of a kick to his jaw.

I didn't understand any of this. Why would Brent do this? Money? I guess it didn't really matter why. He had. Was the virus even real? And Gen? Was that just a lie? But, Lachlan had gotten away. That thought strangely relieved me.

"Addison." It was Lachlan's voice in my mind. I closed my eyes and tried to speak to him, but I couldn't. For whatever reason I could hear him but not talk.

"We know Brent betrayed us. Just hang tight. I will be coming to get you. And if that fucker touches you, I'll kill him. I have to find you first." He was livid and it oozed with every word.

I felt a hand high on my thigh and my eyes flew open. I was staring into the cold eyes of Jack. I tried to recoil from him, but was firmly strapped to the chair, by both wrists and ankles. His hand traveled higher and then he cupped me fully. I turned my head, trying desperately to get him away, but it was all for naught.

Then I snapped. I was so done with this bullshit. Just as his other hand went to my breast, I snapped my head back. The movement caused him to look up and pause, which gave me time to ram my forehead toward his nose and connect with a satisfying crunch. He stumbled back a few steps, holding his now bleeding face. The men stepped forward, but he held out a hand to stop them.

"Addison." It was a nasally growl. His tone alone made me smile. "That was not nice."

"No! What you did to the people in that room wasn't nice. Hell, let's pick another fucking adjective, shall we? How about insane, horrific, monstrous. Take your pick."

"They will be an army. And one that I am being paid a lot of money to create. It's what you people were meant for. To be used."

You people? He spat the words as though he despised pushers. "So, you're just the puppet? Who is your puppet master?" I spat the words, hoping to stall him and, in stalling him, possibly learn something.

"No master. Let's call him a benefactor, though I have never met him. When he saw your file," he licked his bottom lip, the gesture making my stomach turn, "he was very interested in you and he even told me not to turn you."

"Look, kill me or don't, but make your choice soon. I am sure police will be called and this little party will be broken up." My voice was even. I didn't want to die here and not by this asshole, but given the current situation, I really thought it a likely outcome.

"Kill you? No, honey, I'll be turning you. Despite my benefactor's wishes." My blood iced and I stopped breathing. He pulled out a syringe filled with green liquid. "This is the last of the stuff I have made. For now anyway. And as much as I want to abuse your little body myself, I think this is a much better fate."

I focused on the zip ties on my right wrist narrowing my eyes, and I felt it began to give. *Couple of hours, my ass.* I didn't have time to practice with this like I had with the wine. I had one shot at this and the less work, the better. I needed him to close the distance. *Shit, Addison, this is a Hail Mary if I have ever seen one.* My abilities were returning, but I had no idea how strong they were.

He held my arm down and shoved my sleeve up.

"Tisk-tisk. Addison, you were busy weren't you?" he asked, looking at the old scars on my arms. My heart was racing. I took a deep breath in and let it out.

"Jack, don't do this. Please." He only laughed as he

tied the tourniquet around my upper arm, then pressed a few times in the crook of my arm.

I focused on the needle, flexing my power, and could feel the syringe in my mind. I could feel it as though it were in my own hands.

Jack pressed the tip of the needle to my skin, smiling at me as he cooed, "Bye bye, little pusher, see you on the other side."

I pushed my power with everything I had and the syringe flew out of his hand and away from him. I redirected its course so it was embedded in Jack's thigh. He looked up at me with horror and astonishment plastered across his smug-ass face. I only smiled and pushed the plunger filled with the toxic drug, forcing it into his body. He fell to the floor in convulsions.

The five men ran to his aid. It was at that moment I remembered the men had guns and I needed to get the hell out of there. Jack was now foaming at the mouth and his eyes were open and staring in wide astonishment as they filled with blood.

I flexed my power to pop each of the zip ties. Just as the last one released, one of the men caught sight of me and drew his weapon. He fired once and white-hot pain exploded from my left side low on my abdomen. The force of the shot sent me flying backwards. I gritted my teeth at the pain that was laced through my body and went down with the toppling chair, doing a backward somersault and landing on all fours. Two of the four men now had their guns aimed at me. Pusher though I may be, I could still die like every other human out there.

I rocked back on my heels, so that I was kneeling. One hand was by my side and the other gripped my hip. I would have to be faster than I had ever been, and in the amount of pain that I was currently in I gave me less than a two percent chance of working.

I tensed just as they squeezed the triggers. The bullets seemed to freeze in midair and not because of my telekinesis, but because I was moving that fast. I ran to take the guns from the men. Then, with speed I didn't know I had, I found the darts they used on me hidden in one of their pockets. There were four left. I stabbed one in the thigh of each man. I stopped in front of the fifth. I needed him to see me for what I was, not some helpless girl tied to a chair being beaten. He needed to know I was one you did not fuck with. I raised my hand with his gun and pointed it at his head. Then, I narrowed my eyes at the fifth guard and stopped.

I heard the bullets impact the walls. But, I was completely focused on the guard. His eye went wide at the sight of the barrel aimed at his head. He surveyed the room without turning his head. The other four guards had long since collapsed to the ground.

"Addison, I heard gunshots. Are you okay? I'm coming. I had to call for help and get the drug out. I couldn't find you." Lachlan's mental voice was panicked.

"I'm fine," I replied in a cool tone.

Out loud I said, "Hi, I'm Addison. I am someone you really should not fuck with."

The man's brown eyes went even wider, if that was

possible. I distantly heard the gurgles of Jack on the floor. Never taking my eyes off the man standing in front of me, I continued, "Do you get me?" He didn't move; he only narrowed his eyes in challenge. *Oh really, fool?* I tossed the gun behind me and smiled up at the man, who stood nearly a foot taller than me. I was in pain, but fuck it, I was done being seen as a weak-ass female. I was a bad bitch and it was time for everyone to see it.

I used what speed I had left; admittedly it was slower than before, as I was hurt and tired, but still faster than this jack hole. I swiped his feet out from under him, causing him to topple face first to the floor, then I stepped back and waited for him to get up.

"Bitch!" he spat as he got to his feet.

"I'm a bad bitch, but you don't get to call me that. You can call me ma'am," I snarled, breathing heavily. I could feel a gush of blood pour from my wound and run down my stomach. The pain was getting worse, but I pushed it aside, trying to focus on the ass wipe in front of me. *Why didn't I just shoot the bastard?*

He charged me, hoping to grab me around my waist, but I dodged out of his way for the most part. His arm went wide and caught me a scant inch above my wound. It was like being shot again. I almost doubled over with pain.

Instead, I whirled to face him just in time to dodge his next charge, and managed to catch him in the gut with my knee. His breath left him with a whoosh and he fell to the floor. I flashed to him, not giving him time to recover, and elbowed him in the temple, causing him to fall backward, completely knocked out.

"That's Ms. Bad Bitch to you, a-hole." I gritted between gasps of air. Then I did the only thing I could: I fell to my knees and held my wound as though that would help the pain ebb.

The sounds of Jack's transformation had stopped. When, I had no idea, but I glanced at his lifeless form and it was unmoving. I tried to take a deep breath, but oh God it hurt. I gritted my teeth as I tried to get up. Just as I got to my feet I thought I saw Jack move. I froze.

Lachlan threw the door open just as Jack launched himself at me. He never made it to me. Lachlan caught him in midair. Jack snapped his jaw at the air and began thrashing around like an animal. Lachlan literally ripped his head off. The spray of his blood covered my front. I could feel the sticky liquid roll down my chest and arms. The abruptness of the moment caused me to blink, stupefied. One moment his head was attached to his neck and the next it was nearly off. It hung to his lifeless body with little more than a scrap of skin. Both Lachlan and I were covered with gore. He let what was left of Jack fall to the floor in a bloody heap. His fingers and feet still twitched.

I couldn't stand anymore. Everyone had a limit of shit they just can handle and I had just reached mine. I fell to the floor, landing hard on my ass. The impact caused so much pain that my eyes watered.

I must have blacked out because the next thing I

knew I was in Lachlan's arms being carried away from the room.

"Lachlan, how?" It was a rasp. I couldn't manage much more of a voice if I wanted to stay conscious.

"Cannon. I had to call him. The security team was calling the police and Cannon made a charitable donation to several retirement funds."

"Oh, Lachlan, the people. Please don't blow the building." I couldn't stand the thought of these people dying. Being exterminated like vermin. They were people.

"I won't. Let's just get away from here," he said. I thought I felt him kiss the top of my head, but I couldn't be sure.

"What about Brent?" At the name his body went stiff.

"Addison, you've been shot. Let's get you out of here. I can't heal this bad of an injury." His tone was grave.

He carried me out of the room. We were only one hundred feet or so away from the building when Lachlan said, "I am so sorry. But it has to be this way."

I was confused. I didn't know if it was from the blood loss or the fact that my head had been hit too many times, but his words made little sense. That was, until the ground vibrated and rumbled. Lachlan's grip on me tightened to the point of pain. That's when the building's windows exploded and fire erupted from them. The force of the explosion was so heated that my face burned. I didn't try to get away, for I knew with the hold Lachlan had on me and my injury, it was impossible. I laid my head back on his shoulder.

"I hate you." And in that moment, I did.

I thought I felt him flinch, but blessedly my world turned black as I passed out. And part of me wished I wouldn't wake up again.

Eighteen

"**F**UCK, THEO, I HATE THIS PLACE AND THEY WON'T let me leave! You need to come bust me out," I whined.

"The hospital can't be that bad. Free food? Sponge baths? Wait, maybe I will come up there. I'd like to help with that."

I laughed. I couldn't help it, even though the movement made me wince and grind my teeth. "God, Theo, don't make me laugh. That freaking hurts."

"Well, it wouldn't hurt if you took any of the pain meds they have given you." His tone was only half chiding.

"You know I can't." But, oh gosh, I was tempted!

"I know, chickadee. I'll be up there in a little while when you're discharged, but hang tight. Oh, and answer Lachlan's calls." I winced again, not at pain, but at the dull ache his name caused.

"I'll see you later. Bye," I said as I hung up.

My eyes slid closed and my thoughts went to Brent, of all people. It had come to light that Brent did not betray us for money or power, but for love. The mysterious benefactor had his sister. He was threatening to use this drug on her if he didn't hand over information of every pusher he could hack. When he stumbled upon me and this job, he saw it as the ticket to getting his sister back. Turns out, his sister was a pusher.

Unfortunately, it was all for naught. Brent didn't get his sister back. From what I heard, the trail had dried up. Brent tried to trace the money connection, but there were some securities even he couldn't bust through. He even tried to trace the address and phone numbers he had been using, but that had Brent more or less chasing his tail. The fact that the bigwig behind this was just up and gone, like a fart in the wind, made me a little more than nervous. There were bigger fish out there, but they would have to wait. For now, my part was done and I could relax. *Yeah, right.*

Then there was Gen. The information Brent gave turned out to be false. In fact, it came to light he gave the same misguided information to Lachlan. My heart ached for Brent. As much as his actions caused me to be shot, I might have done the same thing for Aaron.

Brent really had created a virus that took out everything in its path. That act alone may have saved his life. But, if nothing else, it proved how much he loved Lachlan and what a tight spot he was in. It destroyed any electronic copies of the drug. Lachlan got all of the physical evidence and Gen and Theo took care of raiding Jack's home. And the whole time, where was I? Sitting in a hospital bed. I felt utterly useless. My bullet wound required surgery, but thankfully, the bullet hadn't damaged much. The pain, however, was pretty impressive.

I glanced down at my vibrating phone. It was Lachlan again. I sent it to voicemail. As soon as he left one, I deleted it. This had become the practice over the last few days. He'd only tried to see me once and I called security to get him out. As he didn't want to make a scene, he left with no fight. Maybe I was being irrational, but damn it he lied to me then turned right around and killed all of those people, even the security guards. What if they had families? Maybe there was nothing that could have been done, but no one even tried. I plopped my head back on the pillow and dozed off a little while.

The nightmares were wreaking havoc on my ability to sleep. One after the next, on repeat, I saw Jack's head being torn from his body and then the explosion, but instead of being outside of the building, I was strapped to a bed. I never died instantly, but burned slowly, able to feel my flesh being burned from my body then healing and being burned all over again.

Somehow, I managed to black out in my dreams and when I came to, I was always on fire. Forever burning. I tried to get away, but in the end, I was consumed until the pain became too great and I screamed myself into wakefulness.

The sound of the latch of the door jolted me awake before I had time to slip into another horrific dream.

"Hi, Ms. Fitzpatrick. How are you feeling?" Dr. Taralynn Stark greeted me, looking down at my chart. Cannon had to pay her and make a substantial donation to the hospital to keep the police out of my apparent gunshot wound, which they were required to report.

"Ah, Doctor Stark. Have you come to release me from my cell?" I replied in a snarky tone. I couldn't help it; it wasn't the young doctor's fault. She looked as though she couldn't be older than twenty-three, but she assured me that she was, in fact, in her thirties. Shoot, I was betting she drew the short straw to perform my surgery and have me as a patient. I wasn't the most cooperative.

"Oh, Addison, it isn't all bad, and you wouldn't be in so much pain if you took the meds I have prescribed you," she remarked as she set down my chart. She walked over to the bed and motioned for me to pull my oh-so-stylish hospital gown up. I did, and I gritted my teeth against the pain as she checked me over with gloved hands.

"Doc, you know I can't take those drugs. I have been clean for seven years. I won't risk it." This fact was more important than ever. The tranquilizer dart must have had some drug in it that resembled something I had gotten high on, because I was having a hard time saying no. My mind kept sliding back to the thought of it.

She finished up and took her gloves off. "Addison,

I know your past, but even some over-the-counter pain meds won't hurt you. I'm ready to kick you out of here and will give you a prescription for some meds just in case. Honestly, I would feel more comfortable with you taking them. But, I can't force you."

Just as I was about to fight her, Theo's smiling face entered the room. God, but I was so happy to see him. He had come to see me every day that I was locked away in this prison. And that act alone kept me sane.

"So, doc, is my girl ready to get out of your hair?" Theo asked brightly.

"Yes, she is. Here is that prescription," she said, handing the small paper to Theo. She continued with, "And I'll call transportation to come wheel you out. I'll see you in a few weeks to take the stitches out. Keep that dry in the meantime. And sorry, no physical activity for at least a month, though I would recommend two. But, I highly doubt you'll listen to me."

"Who, me?" I asked sweetly. That caused her to roll her eyes at me and Theo to choke on a laugh. At this point, I would profess my undying devotion to her if it got me out of here faster.

"Okay, you can go." She waved me off while walking to the door.

I swung my legs out of the bed, grabbed my clothes Theo brought, and headed to the bathroom. Theo never took his eyes off the back of my gown.

"Get a good eyeful. But, keep in mind I haven't had a proper shower in nearly two weeks." He laughed as I walked into the bathroom.

GETTING INTO THE CAR WAS A FEAT OF STRENGTH and acrobatics. Every bend and scrunch of my body sent shooting waves of pain through me. I was in so much pain it took me a good ten minutes to realize that I was, in fact, sitting in the parked car in front of my apartment.

Theo helped me into my apartment and then I told him if he did not stop fussing over me, I would have to hurt him.

I spent the next three weeks healing and avoiding. I avoided Darryl's calls, I avoided Lachlan's calls, and I even avoided Theo. Darryl and Theo showed up to try to pry me from my apartment, but I told them I was in too much pain to leave. That normally shut them up. Yes, I was in pain, but not from that. I never went back to the doctor, so at the two-week mark, I had to pull the stitches out myself. That was a fun task. The worst part was the prescription that I couldn't seem to toss. It sat on my kitchen counter, taunting me.

I just wanted to avoid everything and everyone. Yes, I did realize I was sulking. And, just as I was sulking, I heard my phone ding, indicating a text message. I looked at the display; it was Cannon. *Great, just fucking great.*

"Get your ass here now."

I groaned. He was the second-to-last person I wanted to see right now. But I got dressed in bright-purple running shorts and a matching top. I tossed my shoes on and ran over to his tower. I wasn't as fast as I normally was due to how much pain I was still in, but even then, I realized how much I'd missed running. This was the first time I had run since getting out of the hospital.

I walked into the building and rode the elevator up to his floor. I didn't see the point in knocking, as I knew he knew I was here.

But it wasn't Santa or Cannon who opened the door. It was Lachlan, the last person I wanted to see. I turned and walked back to the elevator. I was so not doing this right now.

"Addison!" Cannon's voice boomed past Lachlan and caused me to pause, but I kept them at my back.

"What?" It was a low, measured whisper.

"We have business to take care of. Get in here." His tone was a warning. I took it as such and stormed past Lachlan, who still had not made a sound. I couldn't help but sneak a glance at him. *Had he lost weight?*

"I was shot about a month ago doing a favor for you. What do you want?" I knew I was playing a dangerous game but, much like me, I really didn't care.

"Addison, I need Lachlan to cut his bonds with you."

I looked from Lachlan to Cannon and both men looked pissed off to the max. I did not want to be here any longer than I needed to be. But, the thought of passing out yet again did not sound very thrilling either. I had been a lot of passing out as of late and I was getting damned sick of it.

"Well, let's do it." Lachlan's eyes flew toward me and they narrowed. *What? Had he expected me to put up a fight?*

"Addison." Oh, but he said my name. He said it like he did the last time, with such power and reverence. It was enough to cause me to rock back on my heels, and for tears to prick my eyes. God, his voice. I didn't realize that it, too, was an addiction. Just hearing it made me want to fall right back in again. I swallowed all the sudden emotion his voice caused and looked away.

I sat on the floor right where I was standing and looked up, not meeting his eyes. I picked a spot just over his shoulder and intoned, "Let's do this," before crossing my legs and waiting.

He didn't move for a long moment, then finally ran a hand over his face and sat down to face me, his blue eyes going cold. *Good, so have mine.* He put a hand on either side of my head. And oh, if I thought his voice was an addiction, his touch was a balm to all of my pain. I would crave his touch when it wasn't there. In that moment, I realized that the cravings I'd felt for the drugs were for him and the comfort he provided. I closed my eyes so I didn't have to look at him. I feared I would lose what little nerve I had left.

"Addison, please. We can figure this out. I know you're mad and hurt, but please fight this. Tell him no." His voice in my mind felt so right. I had to stifle a shudder.

I shook my head. I didn't trust myself to communicate to this man without confessing things to him I had yet to confess to myself.

"I won't do this until you tell me to. I need your words, Addison. I need you to tell me you want this done." I did want this done, didn't I? He had hurt me.

I felt a warm tear slide down my cheek.

"Lachlan, I want our bond broken." Even said mentally, the words carried a sting. And, for the first time, I felt his emotion. His rage, his hurt, but most of all his pain.

I opened my eyes in time to see a wet streak track down his cheek. I felt his mind press against mine and I let go of the last strand of fight against him. Searing pain speared through my mind. My body went stiff and I tried to hold on to consciousness, but it was impossible. Just before I let the blackness consume me, I saw Cannon's dark eyes sparkle and a smile spread across his face. I let go of everything and let the darkness take hold of me.

Epilogue

3 MONTHS LATER

SWEAT POURED DOWN MY BODY IN WAVES, LEAVING me drenched from my hair to my toes. My heart wasn't beating any faster, but it was hammering against my chest. My speed had returned to normal after the events of three months ago. And still, even the mere thought of that time caused me to think of him. Of his voice, of the sound of my name falling from his lips, of his touch, of his kiss, and the feel of his hands touching my...

I mis-stepped and Theo's punch landed on my jaw. It dazed me for a moment, causing me to stumble back a few steps. He rushed over and, in doing so, he caught his toe on the mat, which sent him careening to the floor. Luckily for him, I was there to break his fall. His force caused me to topple to the ground with him landing on top of me.

"Theo, I know you want in my pants, but this is

a bit forward, don't you think?" I asked struggling for breath. I added an extra eyebrow waggle for effect.

"You know I love you, but you're too scrawny for me. I like my girls with a lot more curve than you got. But, if I have to, I guess I could take one for the team," he joked as he rolled off to lay on his back beside me. We both took in huge gulps of air.

I closed my eyes to try to center myself and reel in my wild emotions. I hated that I got like this whenever I thought about him. He could crawl under a rock and die for all I cared. Well, that's what I told myself, anyway.

"Addison." Theo's cool voice was a lifeline pulling me from the sea of thoughts I was currently drowning in.

"Hey, yeah, sorry," I replied absentmindedly. I was always absentminded these days. I needed to shake this off. I needed to shake *him* off. After he broke our ties, he was just gone. I knew the whole thing had upset him, but I hadn't heard a single word from him. I guess that really was for the best.

"You're thinking about him, aren't you?" he asked, staring at the ceiling.

"No, I'm not." I was. Ugh, and I was an awful liar when it came to Theo. He could so see right through me.

"Liar. Why don't you just call him?" It was such a simple question with such a complicated answer.

"It's not that easy."

He rolled over to his side to face me. "Sure it is. You

pick up the phone and dial his number. See easy."

I slapped his chest and reminded, "He hurt me. He lied to me. He didn't even try to save those people."

"Have you ever thought that maybe, just maybe, he did the right thing?"

Now, I rolled over to face him. "Of course I have. But, he still didn't even try. He lied to me so I wouldn't fight him." I hadn't realized just how much pain I was still in until this moment. My heart began to ache with a familiar dull pain.

"How do you know he didn't try?"

I sat up to sit cross-legged. "What do you mean, Theo?"

"Do you know what he was doing while Jack had you? I mean besides trying his best to track you through the maze that was that building?"

"No?" I asked questioningly.

"He called Cannon to help keep the police off his back. And when Lachlan told Cannon he wouldn't kill the turned pushers, Cannon made it very clear that if he did not, he would do much more than kill him. Addison, I gathered that Cannon threatened you, and for Lachlan, that would be worse than death."

I hadn't known any of this. Would it have changed anything? No. I had to hold on to this anger. It made not being with him easier. Didn't it?

"Cannon has sent him on some excursion to pay off another favor. But, he should have his phone. You could call him."

I shook my head. "Theo, this changes nothing.

If it weren't this, it would be something else, or hell. Cannon … or even Merriam."

Theo stood up and offered me a hand up, and I took it. He pulled me into his arms and just held me there. My throat tightened with emotion, tears blurring my vision. I hugged him back and we both just stood there, holding on to one another as though our lives depended on it.

"Let me give you some advice, chickadee. Forget both of them and let me put some meat on your bones, and then I'll put some meat …"

"Ahh Theo, don't go there! The last thing I need is you fawning over me! I have enough crazy-ass men in my life." I prayed he would not finish that last statement.

He laughed, the sound low and deep in his chest as he held me. He pulled back slightly to look down at me. "That punch should have never landed on you. You have got to pull your head out of your ass, because you're going to make a mistake and get hurt." He was right. I knew whatever was going on was a lot bigger and there would be more to come. I needed to do exactly what he said, pull my head out of my ass.

"I love you, Theo," I stated and meant it. Though the words were given to him as a friend, I had never said them to a man.

He squeezed me to him and replied, "I love you too, chickadee." His voice was tight with emotion and he seemed to choke a bit on the words.

We finally eased our hold on each other. He walked

over to the row of chairs that lined the front of the dojo, then picked up his bag and turned to face me.

"Need a ride?"

I shook my head and replied, "No. I'll run home." Then a thought hit me, "Oh hey, how are Gen and Brent?"

"Gen is still Gen. Brent is still searching for the untraceable man. He's in a bad way. He really wants his sister back. I don't blame him, but he's becoming frantic. And the fact that he got you shot about killed him. He is now working for Cannon. Apparently Cannon was pretty livid and did not kill him, because of his computer skills … and because Lachlan asked him not to."

"And Cannon listened? That's new." I remarked, clearly not believing it.

"Knowing Lachlan, I am surprised he didn't kill Brent. But, he didn't."

I made a mental note to go see him and try to help him find the man or faction behind this. There was a small comfort in knowing this was not a government ploy to eradicate pushers. But, like the double-edged sword this knowledge was, it scared the hell out of me that we had no idea who was behind this, nor did we know their agenda.

Theo saw the pain on my face and whispered, "Go home, Addison."

I nodded and he walked out the door.

"Bye, Theo," I called after him.

"Bye, chickadee. I'll see you in a few days. I need to

recover." He rubbed his arms as he walked out the door.

I gathered my things. Since today was a Sunday, the dojo didn't have any scheduled classes, so I turned out the lights and locked up behind me. I tossed my backpack on and ran.

The past three months had been a learning experience in humility, at least where the dojo was concerned. I had to completely open up to Darryl about what I was and what I had been doing. Well, I didn't tell him much about what I was doing other than I owed Cannon. Then there was Kyle. Erica refused to stop her lessons, so we were forced to be in the same room twice a week. I tried to approach him and apologize, but he blew me off. That bridge had been blown to smithereens. For the first time in seven years, I did not look forward to going to work on the days Erica was there.

My thoughts slid to Cannon. He rebound me to him a few days after my ties with Lachlan were severed. He had kept his distance, but I had a feeling that would not last long. Every week, different things would show up at my apartment. Flowers, candy, coffee, all kinds of random things. But never a name. I knew they were from him, as I looked up the prices of some of the shit and my eyes nearly bugged out of my skull. *Was he wooing me? Ugh.*

I pushed these poisonous thoughts from my head and tried to focus on my feet hitting the pavement and the blur of lights as they passed. It only took about three minutes to get home on a normal day, but today was not a normal day. The city was full of people; it took me nearly ten minutes just to get to my front door.

I walked through my front door and right to the coffee maker to get the machine ready to brew its magical goodness, then I went to change. But, before I did, I clicked on the TV and switched to the news station. I walked into my room to change out of my sweaty clothes when I heard what the woman on the news was saying.

"Stay tuned for the six o'clock news. There have been an increased number of rage crimes. People are being attacked and in most cases bitten. These brutal crimes have left a number of people hurt and even some dead. More on that story and others at six o'clock." Cold washed over me. No, it can't be. They were all killed, weren't they? I needed to call Cannon. I had two favors left and I did not want this to add any to that number. I went back into my room to finally get out of my drenched rags. I had just slipped my sweaty clothes off when someone knocked at my door. *But, of course someone would knock right the hell now, ugh!*

"Hold on! I'll be there in a few seconds," I called, hoping whoever it was could hear me. I ran to my closet and grabbed a gray sports bra and black sweat pant and tossed them on. I tried searching for a shirt but quickly gave up when the person at the door knocked again.

"I'm coming. Hold on to your panties." I huffed out as I walked to the door. Whoever it was would have to just deal with the fact that I did not have a shirt on. Hey, it's like a swimsuit, right?

I opened the door and there stood a man with a black suit and tie. He was an older man with a craggy face. It looked as though he tanned far too much. He only stood about five foot seven. But, hey, who was I to judge?

"Addison Fitzpatrick?" he asked, eyeing me with complete indifference.

"Yes? How did you get up here without me buzzing you in?"

"Your neighbor let me in. I have a letter for you. Please sign here." He shoved a metal clip board at me. *I am going to have to talk to my neighbor.* I eyed the document; on it was a sheet that had a spot for me to sign. I took it from him and eyed the paper. Wait.

"Isn't it Sunday? I have never known the postal service to run on Sundays," I asked in a confused tone.

"Ma'am, I work for a courier service. We deliver every day of the week. Please sign the paper." He looked bored and his voice was flat. Clearly, he either had the personality God gave a sea urchin or he seriously hated his job.

I signed the paper and he handed me a letter-sized envelope. He turned and walked off without another word. *Well, wasn't he just a little ray of sunshine.* I tossed the envelope on the counter and poured myself a cup of coffee. I had a feeling that whatever was in that envelope would require coffee to get me through it.

I grabbed a leftover donut and nibbled it as I sipped the coffee. But I never took my eyes off that damn envelope. I mean, for fuck's sake, who sent letters anymore? They could have emailed, called or texted. But a courier service? It seemed so old-fashioned, had this person never heard of FedEx? Or UPS? I snatched up the envelope and fingered the glued flaps, holding it up to the light with hopes of seeing something. I sighed. No such luck.

I opened the letter and pulled out another envelope. This one was tan in color, whereas the one I had just opened was white and had the company name of the courier service on it. I flipped it over to see my name handwritten on it. My heart stopped and I sat it down and closed my eyes. I knew who sent this letter. I knew this handwriting. It was Lachlan's.

I finally took a deep breath and opened the letter.
Addison,

I know a letter is archaic but, when you read this, you will understand. I don't know how to start this, but if you are reading this, I am either dead or missing...

TO BE CONTINUED IN...

Give and Take

book two in *THE VAMPIRE FAVORS SERIES*

PLAYLIST USED TO WRITE PUSH AND PULL

Ella Henderson – Ghost (Addison's song)
Sam Smith – I'm Not the Only One
Stay with me
Latch (acoustic)
Lay Me Down (acoustic)
Ellie Goulding – Lights
I Need Your Love
Lorde – Yellow Flicker Beat
Maroon 5 – Maps
Animals
Sex and Candy
Jesse McCartney – Leavin'
A Great Big World – Say Something
Gotye – Somebody That I Used to Know
Hozier – Angle of Small Death and the Codeine
Scene
Foreigner's God
Sedated

ABOUT THE AUTHOR

Emily Cyr is a stay-at-home mom turned writer. She holds a degree in middle grades education with certification in English and social science. She has always had a love of all things paranormal and fantasy, but it wasn't until Emily's husband said the words, "Why not?" that she considered putting her thoughts and ideas into the book, The Lightning Prophecy. This trilogy was just the start for Emily. It seemed to open a creative door that had been locked.

Emily has always been an avid reader. Through reading came her love of writing. The more she read, the more she knew she wanted to create her own world. Many of her first works were fan fiction.

Emily and her family currently reside in Jacksonville, Florida. She has an incredibly supportive husband who is also an officer in the United States Air Force. They have two sons, ages 2 and 3. Somehow, even with the demands of being a parent to two little boys, she finds time to escape to her fantasies and write them down.

Emily is currently working on book two in the Lightning Witch Trilogy and book two in the Vampire Favors series, titled Give and Take.

All information regarding book signings and release dates can be found on her Facebook page: **www.facebook.com/EmilyCyrAuthor.**

Did you love this book? Please leave a review on Amazon!

Made in the USA
Charleston, SC
18 May 2016